WHO THE
MAN

CHRIS LYNCH

HarperTrophy®
An Imprint of HarperCollinsPublishers

Library of Congress Cataloging-in-Publication Data
Lynch, Chris.
  Who the man / Chris Lynch.
    p.   cm.
  Summary: Thirteen-year-old Earl Pryor is much too big for his
age, and much too powerful for the anger that rages within him
when classmates tease him, the girl he likes disappoints him, or his
parents' problems get too real.
    ISBN 0-06-623938-9 — ISBN 0-06-623939-7 (lib. bdg.)
    ISBN 0-06-441098-6 (pbk.)
  [1. Family problems—Fiction. 2. Anger—Fiction. 3. Violence—
Fiction. 4. Schools—Fiction. 5. Interpersonal relations—Fiction.]
I. Title.
PZ7.L979739 Wj 2002   2002007969
[Fic]—dc21   CIP
                                                              AC

Typography by Amy Ryan
❖
First Harper Trophy edition, 2004
Visit us on the World Wide Web!
www.harperchildrens.com

For Dot—that's my moms

Big Man

RIGHT AND WRONG IS A SIMPLE DEAL, AND
everybody knows it. As long as you have all the facts,
right and wrong make themselves very clear to you.
If you really want to know.

Don't ever be a rat. You don't fink. It's not right. No
matter what, you don't fink, and you don't complain.
It's just not what you do. It's just not right.

And don't lie. Don't lie, don't fink, don't complain.

I try not to complain. But what can you do sometimes? Times like these times. Times like these
days—and these days, they are all like these days.
Deep dark cold night-all-day winter days that won't
give you a break, ever. On these days, I find myself at
school, or on my way to school, before I even realize
that I am awake, that I have gotten up and eaten and

dressed and all prior to finding myself where I am. It's as if I have woken up right on the pavement in mid-stride or in my seat waiting for class to begin, or like I never even slept at all but am still walking through yesterday and the day before because they are really all just one long dark restless winter day that won't give you a break.

Days like that, like these, they just make you feel angry the whole time. Like somebody somewhere is pulling something on you, but you can't quite put your finger on who. And you really want to put a finger on him.

By the time I become aware of things today, I am delivering milk. I am the milkman today. We have a milk program here, and we all get the chance to deliver the milk on a special trolley all around school when it's our turn. The milk company comes by and drops the stuff off at the back door where it sits and freezes in the tiny little cartons that are stacked up inside the plastic-cube carrier crates that are then stacked up on top of each other in a tower as tall as me. It's a lot of milk and a fair-size school, so two kids from our class get the assignment each week, one taking the rooms on the east side of the corridor and the other the west until everybody has milk. It's a chunk out of class time, a bite out of the boring day, so most people love to do it.

I don't. I don't feel like seeing any people today. Now I get to see everybody. At least everybody on the east side of the corridor.

"Well well well well," says Mrs. Sanderson, the first-grade teacher, as I wheel my stupid squeaky cart into her classroom. I always get the stupid squeaky-wheel cart when it's my turn, and I don't know how that is, why that is. Somebody has to be rigging things, and I'm going to find out. They could at least oil the wheels, but they don't. And Derek, who's the other Milk Dud with me, even the law of averages would say that he'd get the squeaky wheels sometimes. But never. And he's always pulling stuff like this. He's never left with the blunt scissors that make your art-work look like you've been biting it off instead of cutting it. He never gets to the pencil sharpener when it's so full of shavings it's puking up curly bits all over the place. These things don't happen to just anybody, and they don't happen by accident. I am going to find out about this. No slipping into or out of any classrooms unnoticed when you have this stupid squeaky cart, and that stinks. I just want to be quiet and unnoticed and go about my—

"Class!" Mrs. Sanderson says with so much enthusiasm you would think the Christmas break was just ahead instead of lying dead in the snow behind us. "Class, do you see this big strapping man right here?"

Of course they see me, Mrs. Sanderson. You kind of made it impossible not to see me even if it was possible not to see me, which it's probably not, even if they didn't want to see me, which they probably didn't, and even if I didn't want to be seen, which I definitely did not.

But I like her anyway. I have liked her all the time.

"*This* fine strapping tower of a man," she says, frog-marching me away from my stupid squeaky cart to the front of her class, "was once right in here, where you children are now sitting. Can you believe it?"

Their innocent little first-grade faces say they cannot believe it. I must look like a tree to them. They must have thought that milk came from trees.

Mrs. Sanderson has an arm around me. That is, she has a hand on my shoulder as she stretches to try and drape an arm over me. She's really little. And really proud. As if she is somehow responsible for the size of me. As if the size of me is something to be proud of, anyway.

"He used to fit in one of those desks like you children are sitting in right now."

The kids all wriggle now, and murmur, stretching around them to look at their own legs under those desks, to try and see their own little backsides on those connected seats. Like there is some kind of answer there, to the physical wonder of me.

"So," Mrs. Sanderson says, giving my shoulder a last extra pat, "make sure, all of you, that you drink your milk up, to grow straight and strong just like big Earl Pryor."

I could break up that stupid squeaky cart, right now, into five million pieces. Break it right over that rat Derek's head.

Like it or not—and the answer is not—I have a job to do, and when I have a job to do, it gets done. But it gets no better.

It almost scares me, the quiet slashed apart by my squeaky wheels in the big open empty corridor of the school. The ceiling is high, the floor is checkerboard black and white, and the silences are silent and the noises exaggerated. I want to be alone, and I can't. I want to be unknown, and I can't. Every step I take, with its accompanying trailing sound track, makes my heart beat a beat faster, makes my hands mad so that they squeeze the handle of the trolley just that much harder, so my own effort is making my fingers redder than even the frozen milk did. My stomach feels so hard and tense you could bounce a cannon-ball off it.

Suddenly I am not alone in the corridor. Out of one of the classrooms on the opposite side of the corridor comes my fellow milkman, Derek. Gliding along smoothly, silently, efficiently, apparently enjoying his job and dragging it out with little turtle steps the way most kids do. He barely takes any notice of me as he heads along, along out of one class and toward the next, squiggling along the wall like a fat-bottomed rat.

I just stand there for a moment and watch him. I stare, silent and motionless, as he goes about his business the way both of us are supposed to. But I am hypnotized.

Eventually he feels it, the way you feel a person staring. The side of his head must have started melting, from the intensity of my stare.

"What?" he asks, exasperated. He has stopped moving, and we now stand there looking at each other from across the corridor.

I say nothing at first, and this makes him more irritated.

"What, mental case. What are you doing?"

I take a breath. The breath does nothing.

So I drive.

I march my cart across that corridor, picking up steam with every stride, the remaining milk cartons rolling around all the new extra space, the wheels squealing madly now, like singing almost, like screaming.

I am at full speed, and full madness, when I reach my destination, reach the west, reach Derek and his wonderful, perfect, silent trolley.

I smash right into him.

He looks at me. Stunned. Speechless.

I back up and smash him again, harder, and this time I hit hard enough to pin Derek to the wall of lockers behind him. It makes an awful racket, but lockers always make a bigger noise than they should. It was not nearly as bad as it sounded.

"This trolley *squeaks*," I say to him.

He stares blankly at me.

The janitor, Mr. Little, comes up from the basement. "What's going on here?" he says.

"Traffic accident," I say.

"Earl," he says in a very stern tone, though he is not a very stern man.

I am about to get in trouble. Derek is not. It is assumed I am the aggressor.

"Derek?" Mr. Little asks.

I look to Derek. We are not friends, Derek and me. We have had our problems. And we will have more. Probably right now, once he opens his mouth.

But here is something. As Derek is there, in front of me, about to rat me out and get me back and win the day, I'm not hating him. I've lost it somewhere, just like that. I don't know where it went to. I don't care.

I take a carton of milk off my cart—which you are not supposed to do. I tear it open and throw it down my gullet, ice needles and all. I wipe my mouth with my hand and wait for it to come.

"We were just switching carts, Mr. Little," Derek says.

Mr. Little's face goes all wide and surprised. Mine wants to look the same but I fight it down. I'm experienced at that.

"Why were you trading carts?"

"One of them doesn't roll so good," Derek says, "so we swap halfway."

Mr. Little is kind of left with nowhere to go. "Oh," he says. "Oh, then. Fine, go on, get the job finished. But don't make any more racket."

He leaves, and we quietly take up our trolleys, our new trolleys. I watch as Derek makes his way to the next classroom on his side. He squeaks now. The wheels wobble and don't want to go quite straight. He pushes on, noisily. I start pulling away, dragging the cart behind me now instead of pushing. It is nearly effortless. It glides, like a toboggan over two feet of new powdery snow.

It occurs to me I *might*, I suppose, maybe *might* have been wrong. About Derek sticking me with the bad cart. I think, for a second, about saying something. I watch him.

But no, he probably did something else rotten already I don't even know about. And he'll probably do more later.

"Hey," he calls before entering another classroom. I turn. "You owe me a milk. For the one you stole off the cart here."

I don't steal. I was going to pay for it. I stare at him long and hard.

I take a carton off my trolley and I throw it, overhand, across the corridor at him. He ducks, and it bounces off the locker behind him. He picks it up, still frozen, unbroken, dented.

"There," I say, "we're even."

I don't know why I should be bothering to think about Derek as I push my way into the next stop on my little odyssey. Derek sure isn't thinking about me. But I am doing exactly that, for no good reason, thinking about saying things and not saying things and doing things and not doing things to Derek, and all the other Dereks, as I slouch my way into Mr. Peppitone's class.

And I freeze there in the doorway.

I cannot believe I am back here.

Mr. Peppitone's class, sixth grade. This is the place. His place. This is where I got big. This is where it happened to me, the awful thing that happened, the strange freakish thing that happened, the growth *splurt* that changed me and changed everything. I practically remember the *day* here, when I outgrew everything.

I am still here, still frozen, still standing in Mr. Peppitone's doorway, being stared at by all the sixth-graders, and by Mr. Peppitone.

The only male teacher in the school. The rooster in the henhouse, big Mr. Peppitone. He stares at me, like he always stares at me. Eyes just like a shark.

He's looking at me, cold fishy eyes, and I'm feeling it, feeling weak. Feeling like I can't go any further. Feeling, at the moment, like I'm too wrong, too little and too big at the same time. Enough.

I reverse, right back out of the classroom.

Teacher wants to know where my trolley is.

"Outside Mr. Peppitone's class, Mrs.," I say.

"Why is it there? And why are you here?"

I am sitting in my seat, as if things were just normal.

"I got dizzy, Mrs."

"Dizzy? Earl, are you sick?"

"I don't know, Mrs. I just . . . I didn't feel too good. Didn't feel right. Felt like I needed to sit down."

There are low-level giggles around the room. I turn, sweeping a look over the whole bunch of them. There is no more giggling.

Teacher sends another kid to finish my milkmanning. I check the big whiteface clock over her head. Nine twenty. Nine plus twenty. The school day is only twenty minutes old. I feel like I have traveled everywhere, the whole school building, my whole school life, backward and forward and inside out, and just wound up where I started, only a lot more tired.

And only twenty puny minutes ahead of the game.

I can't believe how much more of today is still there.

"Do you want to go to the nurse?" Teacher asks.

Don't complain. "No, Mrs."

"Are you sure you're okay?"

"Yes, Mrs."

I do fine in school. I don't love it or anything, but schoolwork doesn't bother me, and so I get along fine. You aren't allowed to talk to anybody when you're doing your work, and nobody is allowed to talk to you. That, I think, is the formula for getting along.

Except today, by lunchtime, I couldn't tell you what I have learned. I've been in there, in my seat, in the class. I've been a body, and I've been no trouble to anybody as far as I recall, but I don't really know what my mind's been doing, because I have retained nothing. This isn't good. It's a school, after all, and if I'm not here for learning, then I'm wasting everybody's time. That's not right. I am aware of it, and determined, if possible, to turn it around in the afternoon. I can do better, I can snap out of it.

I have, in my brown lunch bag, one of my favorite lunches. I sit on the ground outside and peel it open with some excitement, because I can sense it. You are supposed to eat your lunch inside and only come out when you are finished, but the rule pretty much is, if you're not causing anybody any trouble, you can sort of alter the rules in small meaningless ways. If, like I say, you're not doing any harm. At least that's the rule for me. I never see anybody else eating sitting on the asphalt.

Everybody else is running around the schoolyard like a bunch of nutters. Like they have been released from prison for the first time in ten years, even though they are like this every day. It looks like madness all around me while I'm here eating on the ground, but it doesn't feel like it. The wall of sound becomes like no sound at all, and I'm so used to it I'm not sure I could eat my lunch any other way at this point.

It's tuna today, but tuna the way it is meant to be. Because it's been sitting there inside the sandwich for hours, and the sandwich has been snugly wrapped in cellophane, and the cellophane is causing the contents to sweat just a bit, which makes it all come out more flavorful. Light rye bread, just a little bit of mayonnaise mixed with sweet mustard. And chunk light tuna, of course. Chunk light tuna is way better than solid white tuna because it has tons more flavor. They are just snowing everybody anyway, calling it light or chunk, because it is dark, and it is practically shredded, once you get to mixing it. They call it that, I think, because the whiter tuna is supposed to be the better stuff, the fancy stuff, even though it tastes a lot more like nothing, and the big white pieces are so dry they could choke you, and if that's what you go for, then why not just eat turkey instead?

My moms does that sandwich, usually twice a

week. I like the regularness of that. I like the regularness of things, generally speaking. I have a bag of Fritos corn chips. They are for tucking into my tuna sandwich to give it that crunch. Moms would already have the Fritos in there, of course, but that would murder the crunch, and we can't have that. And there's a tangerine. That's all Moms.

There's something else, too. Funny, though, you can tell when my lunch has been tampered with. When Moms does my lunch she uses those brown bags that are meant strictly for lunch bags and come in tight packs of like twenty, so that when you open them up they're like razor-sharp at the edges. Factory-fresh, they are, when she has packed them and then done her neat little one-two-three fold-down thing from the top. But when somebody else has gotten at the bag, you can tell. There's a Kit Kat in there. And there's a Chunky. And a dollar.

That's my dad. He finds my lunch sitting unguarded on top of the washing machine, and he'll open it up and put something in, anything he's got, like loose change or a bag of peanuts, a half-gone pack of gum, one of those travel-packs of Kleenex. Just so that he gets in there. Just so he's had a hand in, my lunch bag, and round about lunchtime I'm knowing it, knowing about him, knowing he's still

there. Then he crumples down the top of the bag all messy-style.

And round about lunchtime, I'm thinking about my dad, and my moms. And there you go. The ground is freezing my backside. But I'm not bothered.

"Hey, there you are," Bobby Norton says. Bobby is my friend at school. Close as I come, anyway. He's a year behind me in class even though he's a year ahead of me in age, even though he's about four years behind in size and looks and the way he acts a lot of the time.

"Here I always are, Bob," I say. "You know that. How come every day you come here and act surprised to see me?"

He stands there in front of me for a few seconds, making a face that I think is supposed to be a scowl. I take the last bites of my sandwich, after jamming in a few extra Fritos. There are some left in the bag.

I offer the last of the corn chips up to Bobby, though just barely up, since I am almost as tall sitting as he is standing.

He takes them, starts munching, resumes talking.

"You went mental and couldn't finish the milk run?"

I nearly choke on a very small wedge of tangerine.

"Where," I say in what sounds like a calm voice,

15

"did you hear that?"

He is rooting around in the bottom of the Fritos bag like a raccoon. "I don't know. You know. Around."

"Around."

"And you stole a milk?"

No more questions.

I throw the remains of the tangerine into the brown bag, which still has the candy bars in it. I jam the whole thing into my back pocket, and I stalk off.

"Hey," Bobby calls after me. "Hey."

I find Derek and his pals at the far end of the schoolyard, around the back of the brick storage building where they play tennis-ball hockey against the wall and the view is blocked from the main building.

I step right into the middle of the game, and the action stops dead.

At first I just stare at him. I'm thinking what I had not been thinking a minute before. I'm thinking about what I was thinking about earlier. How he hadn't ratted when I jammed him into the lockers. Not ratting. Good rule. Never figured Derek to follow it. I was thinking again how maybe I had made a mistake. And how maybe or maybe not I should have said something like that.

I am standing there, and I must be looking funny

or beaming some kind of bad signal because everybody in that tennis-ball hockey game is staring, rigid and waiting, at me.

Probably, now that I think of it, they are staring like that because of the crap that's going around about me. That I'm some kind of nuts or something.

The other stuff, thinking I had made a mistake, falls away again. I step a step closer to Derek.

"My moms didn't raise no thief," I say.

As I say it, the words, my own words, have some kind of effect on me, and I feel myself watering up, like, if I were somebody else I might blubber, but I am not somebody else, so forget that.

My words also have an effect on others. I can feel it. I can almost see it. I can definitely hear it.

Little splutters of laughs people are trying to hold in. Right dead in front of me, Derek lets go.

"Moms?" he says, and spits little rat laughs all into the cold air between us. "Your moms? Momsy? Momsy didn't raise no thief? No, you know what? Momsy raised a giant lunatic," he says, laughing harder with every word, and pulling all the rest of them along with him. "You must have one great big momma there, to be raising such a great big momma's boy."

Momma's boy. That's not right. I'm not *a* momma's

boy. I'm not like that, it's not like that.

I'm *my* momma's boy, though, that's a fact. But it's a fact that's none of his damn business.

Guys will talk about your moms. Generally speaking, that's how it goes, guys talking about other guys' momses. It's a game. It's war. It's supposed to hurt, but it's not supposed to hurt, exactly.

It's what you say when you run out of things to say. It's not serious. It's very serious. It's as serious as it gets.

It's a measure of you. Can you take it? Will you take it? If you will, then what more will you take? 'Cause there's always more. Always more where that came from. If you're going to take it, you're going to take lots of it. You're going to take it forever. But if you won't?

If you won't?

"I was just messing, Pryor! I was only . . ."

It's just not right. Whatever they say about it, it's just not ever right. You shouldn't say anything about a guy's moms. Not ever. And it doesn't matter how many of your boys are around, no matter how temporarily brave or temporarily insane that makes you, you are making a mistake, and you are going to pay.

"*Earl!* Earl, wait, wait. Don't . . ."

And you shouldn't listen to them. Not after they've already done it. Not after. They'll say anything when they're scared, so what they say at that point means nothing at all.

"Come on, Pryor, cut it out. Leave the guy alone. He didn't mean nothing . . ."

And don't listen to their friends, either. Their friends are not people, they are numbers.

It is in stereo then, one voice in each ear, one number on each shoulder. Derek, on the ground in front of me, his head facing down into the asphalt, has gone strangely silent. Funny, the way the mouthy ones go all quiet at times.

But his friends, his numbers, are at me, in stereo.

"Better lay off him."

"Better back off. Better cut it . . . *gooch*."

Gooch.

It means something. Even words that don't mean anything can mean something.

What would you do, if they called you gooch? Do nothing? At first. And then, and then, and then? What would you do then, though? Do nothing? Do something?

Nothing does not work.

Maybe *something* doesn't work, either. I don't

know about that, though. The jury's still out on *something*. But something is all we've got. We must do something.

Kind of strong, these two numbers, these two stereo numbers talking in my ears at the same time, as if together they add up to something. Threatening me and calling me names and telling me what to do and what not to do to people. One of them has his arm locked hard around my throat from behind and it is getting difficult to breathe. The other one, also from behind, is hanging onto my shoulder and onto the hair on the back of my head. They are trying to topple me like a pair of hyenas working a giraffe. My back is strong and I don't buckle, even when kicked in the kidneys. Over and over again.

I don't worry about the numbers. Everybody is caught alone at some point. Everybody has his time. They will have their time.

But this one in front of me, Derek, his time is this time. His time is now.

"What did you say about my moms?" I ask the currently quiet Derek.

"What did I say about your moms?" He is talking into the ground, but I hear him loud and clear.

When they don't go suddenly silent, their memories seem to fail them.

"What did you say about my moms?"

It is at the repetition of the word. *Moms*, the word. I hear the sniggers at my ears again.

What is so funny? That I have a moms? That a big guy with a big fist has a moms? That he loves his moms? Should people find that so funny?

The grip tightens around my neck. Derek turns his head to the side, showing me his profile, trying to get a look up at me.

My fist, as I look at it, is almost exactly the same size as his face. His mean, ignorant little face.

My voice comes out a windpipe-squeezed wheeze, all the angrier for being choked.

"I asked you, What did you say?"

And here's a thing I can almost admire. When a guy is in an almost impossible, dangerous, cannot-win situation. And instead of doing the right, and sensible, and safe thing, he goes the other way entirely, just to show you.

"I *said*," he says. "Your *mother*. Your hairy, fat-ass gooch mother."

I could, almost, admire it, if it wasn't what it was.

I grab as firmly as possible, at the back of his neck, feeling the bunching of neck skin in my fingers, and his hair, and, I hope, his brain stem, as I force his rotten face firmly to the asphalt and hold it there steady while I raise my big right hand, hold it, hold it, shake off the nobodies trying to hold me back.

And I bang it, hard, onto the back of his head. And I bang it, hard, his head onto the ground.

"This can't keep happening, Earl."

"I know it can't, Mrs. Vaz."

Mrs. Vaz is the school's vice principal, and she's all right. And I would know, because we see a lot of each other.

"So, if you know it can't keep happening, then why does it keep happening?"

"I don't know, Mrs. Vaz."

"You must know, Earl," she says, gesturing a little frantically toward the glass door to her inner office. That is where, more or less, we see the *it* she is referring to that cannot keep happening. It is sitting there bleeding through a gauze patch that was recently attached to its mean, ignorant little forehead.

I look away, the other way, toward the window and the snow that has just begun falling. I knew it was coming. I could smell it all morning. It's never far away these days.

"Earl," she says through an exasperated, kindly sigh. "Earl Pryor, you are a test."

"I'm sorry. I don't mean to be a test, Mrs. Vaz. I

don't like tests much myself, so I know how you must feel about me if I'm one to you."

A small tough smile slips across her clenched mouth before she wipes it away. "We are rapidly approaching last chances, Earl. You are going to force my hand."

"I don't want to do that, Mrs. I don't mean to force anybody's hand."

"I know you don't. That's why—for the last time, mind you—I am going to allow you back into class. Once I see you shake hands with that boy, apologize, and assure me that this will not happen again."

Oh no. No. No, please, no, don't ask me that.

I must be staring out the window for longer than I think. The flakes are already so large. They shouldn't be that large, that quickly. But still that's no reason to be rude to Mrs. Vaz.

"Earl?"

Mrs. Vaz is sounding a little impatient with me.

"Earl, it is a mere handshake we are talking about here."

"I know it, Mrs. Vaz."

"Earl? Don't fail to notice how lightly you are getting off here. And likewise don't fail to realize that this *will* be the last time."

From where she sits, I am getting off lightly. She is

being kind to me. I know that.

"Earl? Earl Pryor?"

From what she can see, this is a bargain. Reprieve. Redemption in one quick, painless shake. One hollow apology.

"I'm waiting, Earl."

It is not right to fink. It is not right to complain. So I won't.

But neither would it be right to shake that hand in there. No possible way, no possible how.

Apologize to *that* face?

"What do you say, Earl?"

"I'm sorry" is what I say. "I can't do what you want, Mrs."

She stares at me in a way, a way that's all fat full of disappointment, and that makes me feel bad—for her, but not for him—and I have to look away again, out at the falling snowflakes.

I feel the coldness myself now, feel, in my back pocket area, wet and uncomfortable where the remains of my lunch was all smashed and smeared. The rest of my tangerine that my moms put in there and the Chunky and the Kit Kat from my dad, all of it just smushed. And I feel so bad, like it could just break me, right in half, right now, right from the center of me on out.

But it won't. I won't break in half. It's not going to be me.

Because my dad smokes sixty cigarettes a day, he sounds like Father Time when he talks. That may be why everything he says sounds so important, so big, and so much the truth. That may be why, but I think probably there are better reasons than that.

"You don't want to fight, Earl," he says to me when I come home a little banged up, "and I don't want you to fight."

I tell him I didn't get hurt fighting, that I was just knocked around a little at tennis-ball hockey. That's what I tell him.

"Right," he says through a cough and a wheeze and a cloud of I-don't-believe-you. "You don't want to fight . . . but the other guy might want to. If this happens—"

"It was hockey, Dad."

"If it happens, then you gotta take the fight out of him. If you hit a guy, Earl, you knock him the hell out. It's the only way to be sure. You understand? It's the only way to be *certain* that you don't get hurt. Never assume you're totally safe. Figure everybody to be dangerous, everybody. Be aware. Do not let your guard fall. You do understand me, don't you?"

He is holding my face in his hands right now, and examining me as if he's shopping for melons. There is a butt hanging out of his mouth with a two-inch ash dangling off the end. The smoke is bringing tears to my eyes. Dad's already got tears in his.

His melon head is just as big as mine. But it's screwed onto a much smaller body. It always makes him seem in some way like a big little kid, at the same time as a hard gristly man.

"I think I do, Dad."

"What, think? What's to think about? You have to be sure. Don't think, *know*. You have to know, Earl, that there's gonna always be people who will be out there wanting to clip a guy like you. You're a big guy, a hard-looking guy, and for everybody who's going to be intimidated by that, there's gonna be another who takes it as a challenge."

I am a challenge. A test and a challenge and probably quite a few things more, depending on who you're asking. I would bet I'm the biggest thirteen-year-old you ever saw. I have a hairy chest and I shave. Teenagers ask me to buy them beer at the store. My dad has huge hairy eyebrows that he has to comb up out of his eyes, and I can see already I'm in for those, too.

"I know, Dad."

26

"That's right, *know*. Don't be thinking, be *knowing*. That's my boy, that's my *boy*. Who's my boy?"

"I'm your boy, Dad."

"Who the man?"

"Me the man."

He squeezes my head even tighter in his big bony hands.

He has always checked me over in just this way. He did it back when he had to get down on one knee to do it, and he shows no sign of stopping now that he has to peer ever so slightly up. Always, he has been shopping this melon. He must have always thought the same thought. Melon head.

He finds a lump. It's a new one, and he knows it's a new one, because he knows this surface. It's on the back, just above the right ear, where a little bird was pecking away earlier today.

"Melon head," he says. "You gonna tell me details, melon head?"

I pause. Then I stop pausing. There really is no suspense anyway. "Hockey, Dad. Just like usual, hockey. Hard stuff, Dad, playing ball on asphalt. You know how it is."

Which is not a lie, really. I did get banged in the head during playground hockey, even if I wasn't, strictly speaking, part of the game. When I do play, I always take some shots, more than my share, I think sometimes. The lump could have come from that, if I had been playing, because truly, I don't much notice a lump when I get it, only when it's brought to my attention later. So I can't honestly say it is not a hockey lump. Who can ever say for sure about anything?

He sighs at me. There is smoke in his sigh. He makes like to head-butt me, but instead brushes my sandpapery cheek with his own. "Melon head," he says, going on past me toward the living room, his kite-tail of smoke twirling in the air behind him. "I don't like bumps and bruises on my melon head."

I like the Friday shift. My dad and my moms work totally different hours, usually complete opposite hours, never the same hours. I usually have one or the other of them, rarely neither of them, almost never both. We're always running shifts here.

When Friday comes, I need the Friday shift. When my dad is done work by the time I come home and he's always waiting to check out the melon, and we have the whole afternoon and evening, just the two of us, to do whatever we want, to do whole bunches of nothing, with nobody watching. If one Friday I came home and the Friday shift wasn't on, I think I'd be shook up and backwards for days.

"Come on in here," he calls from the other room. "Come sit down, tell me all about school."

How can I tell him all about school? How can I tell him there won't *be* any school for me next week, that I have been politely invited to stay away?

There will be an almighty fight. It always gets almighty between them, when I've been scuffling.

"Don't you want me to go to the store first?" I call.

"What?"

"It's Friday, Dad."

"Ah," he says, reappearing in the kitchen doorway in a cloud of smoke, his tobacco-brown smile cutting through. "So it is, so it is." He digs out the money.

It's another one of the Friday night pleasures, going to the store for my dad.

"Get me a paper," he says, while he's counting up the money that he has to track down in all different pockets everywhere. He's the only person I know of who spreads his money out in all different pockets in no special order. "And some milk," he adds like an afterthought, as if you can have the same afterthought every Friday after every Friday.

And some cigarettes, I say in my head, but not out loud.

"You okay for cigarettes, Dad?" I ask helpfully.

He thinks about it. He rubs his chin. "Ya, sure, and some cigarettes too."

I do love Friday evenings.

Except once in a while. I don't know if there is a reason, I don't know if God is running things according to any plan or if He lets things happen just completely by coincidence sometimes. But you must give off a smell at certain points. Or a hum or an electrical charge or radio waves. But some days it just seems a guy can't help pulling all kinds of the wrong attention from all the wrong kinds of people.

At least that's the way it goes for this guy, me. And on this Friday. For it is not even four hours since I was suspended from school, and here I am, being a test, or a challenge, to somebody else.

I don't even make it all the way to the store.

"When you turn eighteen, kid . . . I mean the *day*, the *minute* you turn eighteen . . . I'm going to be waiting. You get my meaning?"

I get his meaning. I also get a whiff of everything he had to eat for the last twenty-four hours, and tiny bubbles of spit floating like angry little balloons of hate from his mouth to my face.

This is a brother. Not mine, since I don't have one, but somebody's, though I don't even know whose.

He's probably twenty-two, twenty-three, twenty-seven, big as me. I don't think it was the Derek kid I hit at school. But apparently I had done something not so nice to this guy's innocent brother. And it seems I had done it before. This, I am afraid, still does not narrow it down.

There are some people I don't seem to be able to get along with. And some of them have brothers who act pretty much the same way.

"Because then the law won't protect you anymore, big man." It does not sound like a compliment when he says it. *Big man.* He repeats it, though I'm not sure why. "Big man." It sounds even less like a compliment.

"And someday, I'm going to catch you with no witnesses . . . big man."

He has caught me with no witnesses right now. There are no witnesses here behind the corner store, along the unofficial footpath that leads past the Dumpster, through the hedges, to the ball field and on to my dead-end street.

"There are no witnesses now," I say, just saying it, not to make trouble. Just stating a fact.

Here's another fact, but one I manage not to blurt out. His kid brother deserved it. I still don't quite remember who he is, or quite what I gave him . . . but he deserved what he got.

He looks a little stunned that I said what I said. He goes scarlet in the face and starts breathing heavy through his nose like a racehorse, and the breath's all white and curled, rolling steamy out his nostrils.

I think he thinks the wrong thing. I think he doesn't understand my meaning, and what is not my meaning. I don't want to fight this man. Why would I want to fight any man?

I think this happens a lot. I think people don't understand. People think the wrong things. A lot. When people try and figure other people out, I think they get it wrong more than they get it right.

Speaking has now become difficult for him, where it seemed so easy before. I feel a little sorry for him, he's so worked up. Still hate him, though.

I used to not think that was possible, to hate somebody but to feel truly sorry for them, both at once. Now I know it's possible, because I feel that, exactly that, all the time.

They do a nice job of shoveling around this store. They run things nice. But the snow that won't stop keeps on going, ruining their work, leaving another thin coating that makes it treacherous. I am looking around for where I might establish firm footing, in case I need firm footing. You must always establish firm footing, first, foremost.

"Think you're tough, is that it?"

I am not fooled. That is not a real question.

"You think you're ready, is that it? You think you're so tough, and there's nothing I can do to you?"

I don't think anything like that. But he really doesn't want to know what I think.

"You know," he says, getting sort of calmer and more out-of-control at the same time, "if you take a poke at me first, then I'm within my rights. I *can* defend myself. Maybe I need to defend myself right now, huh, big man? Huh? Do I need to defend myself, right here, right now?"

This is a safe neighborhood. Even at night. Even on the blackest winter night or the sweatiest angry summer evening, anybody can expect to cut through the back of this corner store, or any other alleyway around, and not need to defend himself.

But he's asking me.

Does he need to defend himself?

I just came for milk and cigarettes. I just came for milk and cigarettes, a newspaper and Doritos and cream soda for my dad, and my Friday night video. My dad sent me. But the cream soda and Doritos were my idea. Not like a surprise, though, since the cream soda and Doritos are always my idea. Every Friday night.

I don't want this. Really, I don't want this.

"Well, kid? Well, big man?"

"I'd have hit him," my dad says. He's snatched the unfiltered Camels out of the bag already and is tearing into the fresh pack of smokes. Even though his last pack, there on the table, still has a few in it. He loves a fresh pack of cigarettes, and holds it to his nose after the cellophane is broken.

"You would, Dad? Would you?"

"Well. No witnesses, really, like the guy said?"

I shrug. No witnesses. Like he said.

"I'd have hit him. That is not right, what the guy tried to do to you. There are some things you just don't do—like a man going after a kid. And you're going to find that mostly it's the same people who do all the things you just don't do. So if he stepped over a line and got himself dusted because of it . . . serves him right."

I drop the bag on the table. In the bag is a gallon of low-fat milk, a copy of the news, a two-liter cream soda, the giant bag of Tostitos because I am getting bored with Doritos, and the video *Falling Down*, about a guy who gets angry and goes berserk because he sees things are just not right. We've seen it a few times before, me and Dad.

The bag bangs hard on the table because I have dropped it from some height. Dad looks at me, a bit startled.

I don't like to make a fuss normally. I don't like fussing.

"You okay, Earl?" Dad asks, taking small, unsure steps toward me. He is looking closely now, penetrating me with those eyes he has. Bright green, his eyes, and he turns them on like headlights so that everybody he addresses is drawn to them. They are a lot younger, those eyes, than the beige spiderwebbed skin around them.

I drop into the chair, which looks a long, long way away as I descend toward it, taking forever to get there.

But there I get. And I slump over, let my forehead press into my arm, and close my eyes. I can smell the wood of the kitchen table, and the seep of a lot of different meals, as I breathe, deeply and quickly, over the tabletop.

"Dad," I say as I feel my breathing getting slower, but not much slower, as I feel his hands on my shoulders. "Dad, I'm all tired now. Really, really tired. I'm having a really hard time today, Dad, y'know? And it's making me want to just lie down and go to sleep."

Already I'm feeling stupid and embarrassed, and I want to take it all back. In fact, I try.

"Never mind," I say, trying to stand. "I got us *Falling Down*. Remember *Falling Down*, where the guy wants breakfast at Burger King but they tell him he's too late for breakfast?"

He shoves me back down into the chair before I can straighten all the way up. I am bigger, but he is still stronger. My dad is the strongest man.

He's behind me, wrapping me up, breathing smokey all over me.

"Calm down," he says, and with his Father Time voice he has calmed me, his voice quiet but deep in my ear, his chin dug into my shoulder muscle. "Listen, my boy. You are in junior high, but your hormones are in college. This fact cannot be easy. It will give you some rough times. But these are to be expected—*I've* been expecting them, anyway. At the end of the day, they will be good for you, hard as they are."

I nod. I don't know quite what I'm saying by nodding, but it feels right. And even more, it feels right when my head has to rub back and forth on his head, like cats do to each other.

"Now. Did this guy touch you, Earl? You tell me the truth."

"He never touched me, Dad."

"Good. Next, did you hit him?"

There is a long silence between us. He will let me take my time. He will let me take all the time I need. He always does.

"You don't have to defend yourself," I say calmly to the man. "I'm just here to go to the store."

I take one crisp, military-style step sideways, and move to walk past him.

He jumps in my way. "Says you. Maybe I feel threatened by you, freak. Same as my brother was threatened by you. Mr. Hard Guy. Mr. Big Tough Bullyboy. Ain't got the heart for it now, is that right?"

I take the same sidestep in the other direction. Back to my original spot. I move to walk past.

He is right there again. "Yes," he says, his breathing coming in, coming over me, taking over my breathing. I don't want to breathe him. I don't want his air or anything to do with his air. "I believe I do feel threatened by you," he puffs into me.

"No kidding," I say, and brush right past.

He grabs the sleeve of my shirt.

I turn on him. My hands are up in a blur, and they

are on him. I have him by the collar. I am twisting his collar, and it is choking him.

His hands are up, they are on my arms. But his hands mean nothing.

I am pushing, very hard, and twisting the neck of his jacket closed around him.

Part of me wants to let go. But not my hands.

"I didn't do anything to you," I say. "This is not right, you coming down here after me. You have no business. You have no right," I say, and I drop him.

"No, Dad, I didn't hit the man. I just kind of strangled him a little."

"Well, all right. You need me to hit him?"

"No. Of course I don't need you to hit him."

"Good."

He means that. Good. Good, that nothing happened that needed to be addressed. But more good, that I didn't need him rescuing me from anybody. *Anybody*.

That's the thing, you see. The thing above all things. My dad needs me to be okay, just like my moms needs me to be okay. But he seems to need assurance, some kind of proof, a contract, that shows him I will be okay forever. With him, or without him.

Come what may. That's the *thing*, and the thing is always with us.

"Thing is, Dad . . . I did hit somebody else."

"Oh."

"Yup."

"That's what's bothering you, then. Well, did they deserve it?"

"Yup."

"Then you're okay." First he shakes me, forcing me to pull my head up from the table, off my forearm. He is standing over me now and making a hand gesture like a Father Confessor, wiping away my sins, cleaning me up. "I know you, Earl. I know my boy. You don't hit anybody without a very good reason. I don't question you, Earl. I know, you know. That's all we care about. So just forget about it. We'll watch our movie. We'll eat Doritos—"

"I got Tostitos."

"You got . . . ? Why Tostitos? Don't we always have Doritos? We're Doritos guys, you and me."

Dad likes certainties, better than surprises.

"I got thrown out of school, Dad. For a week."

No more priestlike gesturing. No more shoulder rubbing. It's Dad's turn to look silently. It's my turn to give him time.

My dad is the straightest shooter there is. He means what he says. My father never utters anything he doesn't believe. You don't necessarily have to believe everything my dad says, but you have to believe that he believes it. So when he says that he knows I didn't hit anybody who didn't deserve it, that's the truth. He's not mad at me here, and he's not going to be mad at me. He trusts me. I trust *that*.

He's my dad.

No, this is something else. This pause, this concern, is about another issue, and what to do about it.

And at this moment, she, the issue, joins the scrum.

The phone rings. She calls me every Friday night. She works extra late on a Friday night, usually picking up a whole extra shift in the emergency room. Because she works so late and we don't see each other properly until way into the weekend, since she has to sleep and all, it's always important to her to call me on a Friday night. And it's important to me to answer it. Not that I'd have to race anybody for it.

It rings again.

"The school tried to call but nobody was here. You're going to have to call them, Dad, and let them know you know. Or else they are going to call again . . ."

The phone rings again.

"I know," he says, and goes scrambling through all

40

his pockets for the cell phone he never uses.

I go for the phone. Dad goes for the other room and a smoke, and a chat with Mrs. Vaz.

"Hey, Moms," I say, feeling a little better, then a little sadder at the sound of her voice, at the sound of me bouncing off her. At the sound of the echo of what I've done.

Dad stops in the doorway and gets my eyes with his.

"She can't know about this, Earl," he says in a hush, wagging both his head and his finger.

I nod, because I think I already knew this, and because when Dad says something I nod.

I don't like it. Straight shooters don't lie.

But I know she can't know.

Pryor Church

PRYOR CHURCH. THAT'S MY CHURCH. NOT THE REAL one, the Catholic one, where I go officially for all the church reasons of redeeming and wiping clean the dirty black soul and getting closer to God.

Pryor Church. Where you have to be good already to get in, because there's nothing we can do for you if you're not. Because we are too tired to try.

Pryor Church. It's where I go, in body, when I can get there, and in mind when I cannot. Like when I'm trapped in school, and school is meaning nothing to me, I take a little trip to Pryor Church. Like when I'm in Mrs. Vaz's office and she's saying what Mrs. Vaz says, because she has to say it, like she's said it a thousand times before. Like when I'm home, even, and there are reasons I might like to not be home.

Part of me, an important part, slips off to Pryor Church.

My own church. I found this church.

It's a small, jaggedy, pointy-looking gray granite thing on the edge of an abandoned estate on the edge of an overgrown rotten woods. It doesn't even look properly like a church to me, but more like a gatehouse to some great spooky dark castle beyond it.

It wasn't that hard to find, since it was for sale and obviously wanted to be found. About a year ago, there was a tiny little article in a tiny little community newsletter in a tiny little box on the table at the back of my real church where there are usually fliers about turkey whist fund-raisers and interfaith ski trips to Mount Wachusett.

It was sad. The church was for sale because the owner died.

That was when I first realized you could own a church.

I took the flier, and I hiked out to where they said it was. Kept my nose pointed up and up, into the sky and toward the beacon that is the tallest and most slanted pine tree in the world. It stands, above all the other trees, as if it has a buddy below giving it a ten-fingers-up. I hiked and I hiked. Then I rested. Then I hiked some more, through woods that had no paths, meadows with saw grass spiking up through the snow, and finally through a relentless bed of slop slush so foreign and rich with cold dead-thing soup that I was certain once I reached this place I would be the only living thing around.

I reached it. And I was.

My feet were wet and soppy like giant, cold, boiled zucchinis, and so were my ankles and shins. There were the browned remains of Jurassic-era leaves and insects clinging to my flesh along with crystal ice, and I never felt so badly like I needed a hot bath, but it was soon enough not even noticeable.

There was a NO TRESPASSING sign.

I thought that was either very funny, very sad, or very optimistic for somebody to put it there. Maybe all three.

I liked this church already.

But the place wasn't even locked. Not once you got around to the cellar bulkhead door, anyway.

I felt and kicked and banged my way through the darkened cellar until I tripped on stairs and crawled on up. But even when I pushed through, through the heavy, waterlogged door into the upstairs, I wasn't finding much more. The sun was setting, and there was no real light anywhere. I was aware of the space, of the rooms—both of them. There was the larger part, the main body of the church. It had long oak pews, a small altar, and a high-beamed, steep-pitched ceiling. Through to the back, through another door that was so moisture-rotted that a piece broke off in my hand like a graham cracker dunked in milk, was the second room. All I could tell here was that the room was small, because I could feel the walls close on all sides, could smell the must up close, could feel something, the way you feel something in the dark even though you reach out, reach out again, take a swing at it, even, and it isn't there. But you know it is.

My spine did a judder, and just like that, I was back out.

Back into the church hall, back to the back door. I pulled and pulled at it, then I pushed, then I felt around, found the big four-by-four plank holding the double doors closed, and I flipped it up and sent it crashing across the floor.

The doors opened, and I skittered out. Like a cat.

Like the cat that scooted out right behind me. And the one right behind him.

I stood there in the snow, thinking about taking a breath and going back in.

It was awfully dark all of a sudden. It would take me ages to get back home. I could come back again. When it was light. When I had more time. When I had a light and some good boots.

I could come back. I headed home, turning to look over my shoulder every few seconds for as long as I could still see the place.

That night, I did something that I still think about.

I prayed.

I prayed that nobody would buy that church.

Don't know if that was bad. Don't know if I messed anybody else up, praying for my own stuff, my own wants that may have canceled out somebody else's. Probably. Probably, if I thought about it. But what do you confess? Is there a "Shaltnot" pray for selfish things? There should be, I suppose.

That was a year ago. Now, when I stand in the Pryor Church, it really is *my* church. My sanctuary.

I have pulled the plywood off several of the rocket-shaped windows that are way up high on either side, and now there is light. Not so much light that you feel out in the open, exposed to God and the elements and who or whatever else might get the idea to swoop in and shatter everything. But enough light. Enough light, and enough shadow. To see. And to not see.

I am not afraid here anymore. Ever. Even if it's dark. Even if it is stormy and wet and maybe even unhealthy. Sometimes, even, I come here deliberately, when the sky is crashing and you all but need a canoe to get here, and a kayak once you're inside once the snow melts. I love it here. I love my church.

It's not a church proper, though, which is important. Not a real one, not *the* real one. I worried about that for a while, worried that God was going to get angry thinking I set up shop on my own, until I realized He couldn't possibly think that of me because He knows me. And because anyway, whatever kind of church this even was before, it's not even that now because the plug has been pulled. The juice was switched off when the previous owner went off to meet the Man.

I don't know if I would want to be him.

So it's not a church, exactly. Though it is.

I stand here, at the head of the church. On the altar. To the side of the altar, up the six curving stairs into the sort of preacher's tub suspended high above the congregation, above the world.

I stand here, and I look out. Over the imaginary congregation. I try and imagine his congregation.

Try to imagine my own.

I could stand here for an hour, looking out. I know this from experience. Could stand here for four. I know this likewise.

After the first hour, I am floating. No, I do not *feel* like I'm floating above the flock because the platform

47

holds me high. I *am* floating. Weightless. Heightless. Bodyless. Lifeless. Unreachable.

"I love you," my voice says from the back of the hall.

"I love you."

Dad never ever let me win. We would wrestle, he would win. We would shoot baskets, playing twenty-one or horse or whatever game he could devise on the spot, he would win. We'd throw horseshoes, or pennies, or punches. He would always win.

Just barely, sometimes. But he would win. I came close many, many times, closer and closer with every pound I gained, yet in the end he had no shame in working up a devilish, smelly sweat to beat me. Still he beat me.

It was, and is, just his way. Because he loves me.

"I love you," he says, and it's burned into me. He is sitting on me, a panting, gasping old man, a sweaty man, smoker-man breath all over me, as if to finish me off with the fumes. The only reason I understand the words at all is because I heard them so many times before, because they are not real words at all. They are the shapes of the words, the friends and neighbors and shadows and memories of the words. *I of eeou aanyou no't.*

"I love you and you know it. You understand. And that's why I cannot let you win." *Haffta wanna beet-mee. Hafftabeetmee.*"

"Have to want to beat me. Have to beat me."

The shapes and shadows of the words I know so well. And the smell. The nicotine-rich soap bubble that carries all of Dad's words, floats them on the air until they land, *pop*, to break open on the tip of my nose and I get his message, and maybe some more messages that he didn't intend.

He falls over, falls right off me onto the floor, where he spreads himself out to maybe absorb more air through his pores by opening himself up like cross-Jesus, and he begs me to get his cigarettes.

And I will, of course. I will and yes, I will get the cigarettes for my dad, and I get to my feet with some difficulty since, after all, even though he had to practically kill himself to do it, my dad has given me again a whipping to remember. I remember as I roll onto all fours, and push the floor away from me, and creak all the way up tall, and shake my head.

And find my moms standing blocking the doorway to the kitchen.

She looks like I don't know what, standing all strong and brilliant, filling the doorway with her white nurse outfit and scowl that smiles for a tiny bit of a second at me before going back into scowl again.

I lean ahead and kiss her cheek. I pull back and see my sweat glistening on her skin, and I see it there, just the palest baby swatch of what can only be my own blood from the corner of my own mouth resting very near the corner of her own mouth.

Not one bit. She isn't going to like this, not one bit.

"Hey, Moms," I say hopefully, where there is no hope.

You never saw a man move so fast. You never saw a near-dead, wheezing man move so fast. You never saw a man move so fast and at the same time try to try to *look* to be not making any big deal.

There is no dining furniture in the dining room, where Dad and I had been wrestling. But there are two doors. Moms stands firmly in the one that leads directly to the kitchen. Dad exits through the one that leads to the living room, then the hallway, and eventually around to the kitchen and the cigarettes. We, all of us, *the household*, wait. There is a sound to come, a trinity of sounds, before we can re-animate.

Shhhik. The striking of the match that lights him up.

Clop, clop, clop. He is to the door.

Bang. Three become two.

She came home unexpectedly. She is not supposed to come home unexpectedly on a Friday night. Nobody is supposed to do things unexpectedly around here, not even come home from work way early and make me a fine supper and do some mothering on a Friday night for a change. Things get all off tilt when somebody does something unexpected.

He'll walk around the block now. Maybe around and around, orbiting our neighborhood until the gravitational pull is finally snapped and he floats off into I-don't-even-know-where. Good for his lungs, though. Good for him, I suppose.

Sometimes I have a thing, a thing that might hurt a lot or a little or possibly not at all, but that looks like pain. Like a black eye, or scratches diagonally across my face. But I'll say they are something other than what they are because that's what a guy should do. No bellyaching. Mostly what looks like pain is a lot less pain than people think anyway, so it's not so hard to talk it off.

Then there's the opposite side. The way it goes mostly, is the stuff that is not out there in public view is the stuff that hurts. That's the stuff that hurts like mad.

A stabbing jab way down deep in the side of the stomach is that kind of hurt. What do you do with that kind of hurt?

I have a stabbing jab down there. It comes, and it

goes, and I don't know why and I don't know when, but I do know it will come again. It comes a lot; a lot more than it used to.

"Talk about things, Earl," Moms says. "It's better when you talk about things. You feel better."

My moms looks like a sweet potato. Kind of pinky-red and kind of rounded at her edges.

She *is* a sweet potato. Dad used to say that all the time. *My sweetie sweet potato*, he would say.

I have a pain, a stabbing jab way down my side. Below the belt.

There. I told you about it, didn't I?

Doesn't feel any better.

So why bother? So, why.

"Nothing to tell, Moms," I say while I watch her pop potatoes into the blender. She boiled them yesterday. If she can't make me a wonder meal all at once, she will take the parts of several days to do it.

"Everything's okay?" she asks as if this hardly seems possible. She is a nurse. She has a nurse's nose, and probably reacts that way whenever anyone is just okay.

"Everything's okay, Moms," I say.

She has tears blubbing up under her eyes as she pops onions into the blender on top of the potatoes. Bermuda onions, then scallions, then leeks. Then whole cloves of garlic. Then carrots. One yam, and one beet for mad color. Milk. Butter. Salt and pepper.

The blender sounds like a cougar fight.

Every corner of the house smells like you want to go in there and lick the buttery walls.

"Tell me something," she says as I attack the enamel of my bowl by trying to scratch up every last hearty soup drop with my spoon. It's an awful habit, even annoys me myself, but I can't seem to stop it, and at least it serves as the official end-of-meal signal.

"What?" I ask.

"Are you as silent with him as you are with me?"

I put my spoon down in the bowl, and look Moms in her eyes that used to be the color of jay feathers but are now the color of pigeons.

I shrug.

She sighs.

"Do I have to wrestle you all over the floor like he does, to get conversation out of you?"

I think about it. I can picture it. This makes me smile. So I do.

This makes her smile. So she does.

And this will do, for now. This will do nicely.

Later, after a quiet dessert, a quiet movie, and a quiet walk upstairs, my moms comes to tuck me in. She still comes to tuck me in. Even if I've been in bed for hours, if she comes in from work in the middle of the night, she'll come in to me. As much as Dad likes me big, wants me bigger, Moms prefers me small. She'd like me to go back to little and stay right there, where she could wrap me up and hold on tight until all of time.

Sometimes I think that's not nearly a bad idea.

And then some days I feel so strong. I can surprise myself with it on these days, days when I wake up and start stretching out and look at my feet that seem to be further away from me already than they were yesterday. And I stretch out, stretch the arms and the legs, stretch out my big hands like you would if you were trying on a brand-new stiff pair of leather gloves. And I look at this hand and I say, Lord, hand, where did you come from?

And I make a big ol' fist out of it.

"Hi," I say softly into the darkness when she is there. Her warm breath is brushing nice over the spot above my right ear. She has found it, my new lump. Found it in the dark, without any tell-tales from me. She has sonar like a bat that brings her to my hurt places if I don't cover them way way up.

"It's nothing, Moms," I say, and I say no more.

Nobody asked me if I wanted to be big. I just got big. Or rather, big got me.

In Sevens

SATURDAY'S THE DAY WHEN I CAN'T FIND MY WAY.
More than the other days.

Because Saturday has no bones, no structure. A guy needs bones.

"Earl," Moms says in my ear. I am sleeping. I can hear her, but still I am sleeping. I am always sleeping until somebody, one or the other of them but never both, wakes me up. I like to be woken up, by either one.

Waking up and going to bed, the first person you see and the last person you see, that is what you wind up feeling. That is what adds up to more than all the other hours in between, somehow. For me, that's what lingers. Seeing the face, hearing the voice, feeling the breath, smelling the skin, in those minutes when you're falling out of the world, or when you're climbing back up into it. It really matters to a guy, who's there. It really lasts. And I'd say it goes about four-three, or three-four in the average week, how many times I wake up to my dad or my moms but not both. Four-three, three-four is all right. It's fair and even. Or anyway, as even as you're ever going to get in a life divided in sevens.

Moms, when it's her turn, does it so soft and sweet. Like a fairy. Like a fog, she floats into my room and before I know it she is there, at my side, at my ear, even touching, ever so lightly, the crusty curvy outside bit of my ear.

"Earl," she says again softly. I feel her breath on my eardrum. "Earl, Bobby's here."

"What? What, Moms?" I haven't climbed all the way back up yet. Not fully into the world. Not fully out of the other one.

"Bobby, Earl. Bobby Norton is here for you."

Bobby. Right, Bobby. Of course, Bobby. Bobby is the closest my Saturday comes to structure. Bobby is Saturday's version of bones.

And Moms is happy to tell me that Bobby Norton is here. Moms loves Bobby Norton.

"Bobby's here," I repeat in order to make it real.

"Bobby's here," she repeats in order to help me.

"I'm here," Bobby's small thin voice says from somewhere down the hallway.

I look at the clock. Moms hovers at my ear. It's a kind of ridiculous arrangement probably, the kind of pose a photographer would force people into and that is completely artificial. Except that it isn't. It's all true.

We look at the clock together, me and Moms, and we see together that it is ten past twelve.

I do sleep too much. I know I do. But if I had half a chance, I'd sleep more.

"Thanks, Moms." I say.

She straightens up. "Will I send him in?" she asks.

"No," I say. "Keep him with you till I get ready."

She's happy to do it. Like I say, Moms loves Bobby. He's everything she would want in a son.

I lie. She has everything she wants in a son, because everything she wants is me. What I mean is, Bobby is everything *else* she would want. Everything I can't be.

Bobby is small. He is weak, and he is gentle. He has soft little hands and a whispery voice and perfect manners kind of like a scrawny dog that throws itself on its back at the first sign of threat. He has never been in a fight in his life and will probably never be in a fight in his life and therefore, the Bobby Norton you send off in the morning is likely to be the same one you get back at the end of the day. Unaltered, unmarked, undamaged. Mothers like that.

He is also a very good friend. Good thing, since he's the only one I've got.

"Hey," I say when I come to collect him from Moms.

"Hey," he says, slapping closed some catalogue or other that Moms is dragging him through. She consults him on stuff. My birthday is coming up in another month, maybe two, and so plans must be made.

"You want to keep him, Moms?" I ask. "Or can I have him now?"

Bobby cuts in, his voice an excited dog whistle. "You want to keep me?"

"Of course we do," Moms says. "Who wouldn't love to have you around all the time."

"Ya," I say, grabbing him by the back of his shirt, "who wouldn't."

"What are we going to do, Earl?"

"Walk around, I guess. That's what we usually do, isn't it? On a Saturday? We walk around. Then maybe we'll bowl a string. Then maybe we'll walk around some more."

I hope not. Even the walking we are now doing is depressing me. The buildings all abused and beaten and coated with frosting from the endless sideways blowing of snow and ice.

"That's not what I mean. You know that's not what I mean."

I sigh. Of course I know.

"I mean, what are we going to *do*?"

"Well, Bob, there's not a lot of question to it, is there? You, you're going to go to school, and I am not. I'll keep busy. It's only a week, after all."

"But *me*, Earl, what about me?" Bobby has flipped around now, is walking backwards and bouncing up and down in front of me as he talks. There is a sad droopy look to his eyes, because he is taking this thing very seriously.

"Like I say," I say, "it's only a week, Bob."

But it's not only a week, is it? Nothing is that simple anyway for regular folks, and for sure nothing's that simple for little Bobby N. Just like he's the only friend I have at school, I am likewise all he's got. Only, not likewise. More-wise. Because I can get by. Truth is, I'm not all that interested in friends, which goes a way to explain why I don't have them. Most people, from what I can see, are kind of crap, so why get involved.

Bobby, on the other hand, is friendless because God pretty much designed him that way. He's really small, see, and he's got that voice, like I said. Even when he talks right at you, you might think he's being all secretive and talking trash about somebody really sneaky-style. He looks, actually, like a little wallaby, with a bottom half bigger than his top half, long skinny feet, little stunted arms, and a bitty gray head and ears set way up high on it.

All of which shouldn't even matter to the way he gets treated by people. But it does.

Because people are what? Right, we know what people are.

And it is not right, by a long shot, the way Bobby gets treated.

But he doesn't get treated that way when I'm around.

"Earl?" Bobby asks, a little more urgently as I lengthen my stride and pass him by. "What about me, Earl?" he says, beating feet to catch up.

I don't exactly have an honest answer for him. That's why I say, "You'll be fine, Bob."

I need two liters of cream soda before we do much of anything, and Bob will need a juice box. We head for the corner store like always, like clockwork and tides and anything else that happens all the time just because it happens to happen. We need to do things just about the same way all the time. Or at least that's what I need, because I am what they call a creature of habit.

It's the same store that I go to for Dad on Friday nights, that I go to probably three times a week for Moms, and that Bobby and I go to every Saturday for our cream soda and juice box. We are so reliable that if the FBI or somebody ever needed to track me and Bob down, all they'd have to do is stand around the cold drinks section for a while and there we would be.

But unfortunately it's not the FBI that wants us.

"Gooch," the voice calls out, and I practically squeeze my eyes shut.

"Yo, man. Just the man."

"Ya," I say. "Hi."

I try to walk past. There are about five of them. I don't know them by name, or not really, anyway. There's a Wayne, I think, a Barry, a Clifford. I hear them talking, I see them around, but they don't mean anything to me. They are all a lot older than me, fifteen, sixteen, seventeen years old. There are a few girls with them, too, and I don't know any of them.

Except one.

"Hi, Earl," Louisa says as she comes right up close to me. I stop short. I wanted to walk on by, still do want to walk on by, but cannot. This is Louisa.

"Hi, Louisa," I say.

"Where you going, Earl?" she asks, but that's just stupid. It's obvious where I'm going. I'm going into the store.

"Nowhere," I say.

"Well why don't you hang around awhile."

I hear a chorus behind her. A chorus of Waynes and Craigs and Tonys and what-all, all wanting me to hang out.

Right.

"Sorry . . . no . . . can't, Louisa. Sorry, no."

Somebody is booing me. This is really stupid. Nobody wants me to hang around, so why don't they just shut up.

"Come on," the blond guy says, stepping up closer to me, closer than Louisa. The guy who called me gooch. "Come on, we want you to hang out with us."

"No thanks."

Bobby has scooted right up behind me, like practically pressed against my back as if he's hiding behind a wall. There is a slight tugging back there, and the wispy sound of his voice, as if I am the only one who can hear him. Which could be true.

"Oh, Bobby, hi," Louisa says. "I didn't know you were back there."

"I am," Bobby says.

"Is that why you can't hang?" Louisa asks, all warm and understanding as if we are discussing some embarrassing gross medical problem I have. "Because it's cool. We're cool. He's cool with us."

"He's cool with us," blond Wayne chips in, followed by a splattering of other "cools" from the crowd.

"No," I say, "that's not—"

Bobby tugs. I turn.

He's nodding.

"Shut up," I say.

"What's the matter?" Louisa asks.

"Nothing," I say.

"Why not?" Bobby asks.

"Ya, why not?" the blond guy asks.

I turn and glare at Bobby. "They don't really want us here."

"Maybe they do," he whispers.

"Sure we do," the blond guy says, and pats me on the shoulder.

My right hand fuses instantly, into a fist.

I turn and look at him. I have on a face, I know which face. I feel it, but it is involuntary, and beyond my control. My head is tilted sideways, my eyes are squinted so I have lines like a forty-year-old snaking all over my face, and my top lip is peeled back over my teeth.

I see him recoil, just a safe little bit.

"Sure we do," comes Louisa's soft, familiar voice. She grabs both of my forearms in her little hands. "We want you to stay awhile."

My fist opens like the head of a big fat flower. My face relaxes.

We will stay awhile.

"Awhile," I say. "Then we really have to go. I have things to do."

"Of course you do," Louisa says brightly.

So we stay. Not that it makes any sense. Not that I want to be here. Not that they really want me here. I stay for Louisa, I guess, which is a stupid enough reason, and I stay for Bobby, which is even more ridiculous.

"Why did you want to stay here, with these guys?" I ask him when we have settled into our spots. Our spots being the side of the Dumpster by the side of the store, where we lean. We aren't doing anything we weren't doing before, we aren't with anybody we weren't with before. We have just accumulated here, drifted here against the building the same way random trash always does, the same way snow is now drifting, banking up, threatening to bury us. It is colder now, because we have stopped, and it is suddenly lonely. I feel more isolated, being here, than I felt when I was going along on my way with Bobby.

"Really, have we got a reason to be here, Bob?"

"Why not?" He shrugs.

"'Why not' isn't an answer."

"Because we were asked."

"That's it, Bob? You spend your time with somebody just because they ask you to?"

He pauses, nods. "Ya, that's basically the way I run it, Earl."

"That is deeply sad. And not sad, as in it makes me sad, but sad as in *sad*, lame, pathetic."

"I don't care," Bob says coolly. "Sad it may be, but I can promise you it doesn't wind up with me turning people away, or double-booking in my calendar. Anyway, it's nice to be wanted. Don't you think it's nice to be wanted?"

"We're not wanted."

"You don't *want* to be wanted, Earl. That's the difference. I really want to be wanted."

"Sad."

"I don't care. I think we're making friends."

"Look, nobody's even talking to us. We could be

bowling or something."

"Ha, you're wrong. Look."

The blond guy has decided to pay us another spot of attention. He has splintered from his pod of guys about ten feet away from us, and is grinning like a politician.

"I'm Wayne, by the way. Did you know that?"

"No," I say.

He shakes my hand, turns and shakes Bobby's little mitt.

"Hi, Wayne. I'm Bobby."

"Right, well, what are you guys drinking? I'm buying."

"Really?" Bobby asks. He's sounding like a kid, a completely spazzy kid, and he's embarrassing us.

"Really?" I ask, far calmer.

"Sure. What'll it be?"

All right, I figure, might as well test him out. "Two-liter cream soda."

"Two . . . ? Ah, well, you are a big 'un, right? Big 'uns gotta fill up. Sure."

Wayne is already walking toward the front entrance of the store when Bobby calls out, "Jolt cola, Wayne."

Wayne waves at him without turning back. We continue to watch as he walks into the store, and we continue to watch, like dogs waiting for their masters, afraid they won't be coming back out.

"Jolt cola," I scoff. "What happened to your juice box?"

"Jeez, Earl, I can't be sounding like a complete *kid*, can I? You want to be invited back, or not?"

"Not, I think."

Bobby is shaking his head at me, like he's disappointed, disgusted. "You better snap out of it, Earl. You better start trying to like people a little better."

"Ya? Why's that?"

"'Cause you're gonna wind up with nothing but me, that's why."

I turn to laugh with him, and give him a short shot on his short arm.

But he's not laughing. Not smiling, even.

"Here you go, young men," Wayne says when he has come back with the goods.

"Thanks a lot, Wayne," Bobby gushes. "Thanks, really, a lot."

"You're welcome, really, a lot," Wayne says, backing away, laughing a little.

I nod my thanks. He nods his You're welcome.

"How cool," Bobby says.

"Jeez, Bob, he didn't buy you a pony. He bought you a cola." I grab his drinking hand. "And it's not even a

Jolt, it's a store brand."

"Oh, wow, I guess I should send it back, then."

"Maybe you should," I say. Then I call, "Hey, Wayne—"

Bobby jumps me, which is a scene that always makes me laugh. He's all arm and leg, trying to reach up and grab at me and kick me while trying at the same time to preserve his precious not–Jolt cola from spilling.

"All right," I say, "all right." I don't even have to go to any trouble to defend myself beyond just straightening up a little. He mostly just bounces off me a couple of times, then tires, then sits down on the little curb that runs along the brick side of the store building. I sit down next to him.

For their part, the older kids don't seem to do much worth doing, but they do it on and on, and with great enthusiasm. They make comments to each other that are supposed to be funny and probably dirty—I can tell by the way the speaker always laughs first, and hard, and then punches, shoves, or bear-hugs whoever he's talking to. Sometimes one of the girls slaps one of the boys on the arm, or squeals in a way that doesn't sound like she is really offended at all. They throw coins against the wall. They throw plastic bottles and candy wrappers right down onto the ground,

but keep it all in a contained pile as if they are helping somebody out by keeping their filth tight. They
make comments to practically every person who
comes in or out of the store, and almost nobody
responds to them.

We go about twenty minutes without being
spoken to. I am finished my cream soda. Bobby has
worked through half his cola, and his hands are
already shaking.

"Let's go bowling," I say, grabbing one of his wrists
to stop his jittering.

"Okay," he says, sounding both wired and deflated
at the same time.

We stand to go, and this brings Wayne over like a
mosquito to a bug zapper.

"Where you going?" he says, all serious. "Don't go
yet. We're just starting to have fun."

"We are?" I say doubtfully.

"Are we?" Bob says hopefully.

"Sure, sure, sure," Wayne says, and I feel it. I feel it
in the salesman's way he starts repeating himself. In
the buddy-buddy of the change in his tone of voice.
And mostly I feel it in the curious decision he has
made, to put his arm around my back.

The outline of his hand feels like electrodes
patched onto my back. Like a palm-shaped series of

shocks, or deadly sharp needles. I spin away from his touch.

"Okay," Wayne says, "well, the thing is, we need to start having more fun, we need to boost the party a little bit."

"Boost the party," Bob says, like a little cheer. He raises his bottle, his hand twitching with it.

I fold my arms. I say nothing. Here it comes. I don't know for sure what it is, but I know this is it.

"See, big man . . ."

Gooch is better. When somebody calls me gooch, I can figure them. They are crap, but they are crap up front, around the back, and straight through. Big man, though. Big man, or the Man, or my man . . . those are the worriers. Those are the ones, the ones that sound like compliments, the ones to be suspicious of. Compliments are where evil hides.

"You're the man, big man." Wayne pulls a crumply bunch of dollars out of his pocket. "There's a new girl in there at the counter, I noticed. I noticed when I was in there buying your drink. How was that cream soda, anyway? Good? Good. You're a thirsty guy. And y'know, we're . . ." He gestures broadly toward his bunch, who are intensely pretending not to be paying attention to us. "We are also a thirsty bunch of guys."

He has paused, but I know he's not finished. He is leaning in closer to me again. His head is tilted to one side, and his hand is reaching once more for my shoulder.

". . . And gals," he says, with a chuckle and a wink and a squeeze this time, of my upper arm. "Louisa, right?" he adds unnecessarily. "How 'bout Louisa, huh? You know Louisa, right? She's a neighbor of yours, right? Ya, sure, we all know that. She told us. You know that, that she told us? She talks about you, y'know."

"What?" I say, so anxiously that I make Bobby sound cool. "What? Louisa . . . what? About me?" I try to get it together. I pause, I think. Make sense, Earl, make sense.

Too often, I can't make sense, if it's Louisa. She's not like other subjects. She's not like things I can figure out and know what's what. I can know things. I am not just big, really. I have eyes and ears and a brain to work things out, and I do work things out. I understand, right? And I am not often fooled by stuff. I don't allow myself to be fooled by stuff. I am sensible, almost all the time, and I am proud of myself for it.

Almost all the time.

"She doesn't talk about me," I say, a desperate

attempt to get it back when I've too plainly lost it.

"Yes she does," he says confidently. "Don't you doubt it, big man."

"Excellent, Earl," Bobby says. "A *girl*, man. And a really great old girl."

I look over to the crowd, to where Louisa is looking, at me. She is looking at me sweetly, warmly, with a wide-open smile and a little miniature wave like it's something private nobody else is to see.

"Now what we need, big man, is for you to go to that new girl behind the counter, who won't know you from nothin', so you won't have any problem. And I want you to get for us two twelve-packs of malt liquor, and a fifth of vodka. You can do that, huh? And the cheap stuff, right? Don't go wasting our money on some nice fancy bottle. If the label looks like they made it themselves in the store, that's the job right there. Got it?"

I get it. I sigh.

Sometimes I think I know so much. Sometimes I look in the mirror and I believe what I see. I believe I am the big man. I believe I am as old as the guy I see and I know stuff and I can't be fooled.

And then it happens anyway, and I remember, and I make a note never to let it happen again.

I feel my face with my fingertips. I haven't shaved

today. I didn't shave yesterday. I know I look like Wolverine. I know I can do this.

"I can't do this," I say, and brush past Wayne.

I think Bobby is more disappointed than anyone. "Yes, you can. Sure you can. Wayne, he can."

"No, I can't," I repeat, and march on, with Bobby pulling on my shirttail.

Wayne catches up, joins Bobby in tugging at me. I stop short, turn, and smack away hands. I don't care whose they are.

Wayne doesn't care, either.

"Hey," he says, a bit of new, unpleasant, unphony edge to his voice. I actually like it. "Big *man*," he says, and even that sounds different. Less complimentary, more right. "Aren't we friends, big man? We're friends, aren't we?" He tries to stuff the bills into my hand. I leave the palm open, rigid and flat.

"Ya, we're friends, Earl, right? Earl is friends with us."

Sometimes I'm near to losing my patience with Bob. I want him to be smarter. I want him to take care of himself better and be less of a chump.

But he's not there, and he might never be there. He can't hear what I hear, that when a guy like Wayne insists he's your friend, it sounds like you are being threatened.

I shake my head. "Sorry, no, it's just not right. Can't do it."

I go to leave again, and somebody tugs at me once more. I don't look to see who, but whoever it is gets a royal smacking across the hand that I'm certain leaves an angry welt. It doesn't even matter who it was because they are both the same. They both want to pull me, they are both the same. They both want me to go in and buy that stuff, they are both the same.

I have reached the street, at the lights, and crossed already by the time I hear it.

"Wait. Earl, come on, wait."

No, please. Not this.

I turn it up a notch. I can cover two whole pavement slabs at a time without even running.

"You know I can't catch you, Earl Pryor."

There it goes. There, she's done it. Earl and Pryor together. Earl and Pryor and Louisa—or Louisa's voice anyway—together. It's a spell. An incantation that leaves me without strength or will. Or sense.

I stop.

"Just this once," Louisa says.

"You shouldn't do this," I say.

"Oh, Earl, don't be such a prig."

"You're too young."

"I'm a lot older than you."

"Well I'm a lot too young."

"Please."

"And it's too early in the day."

"Jeez, *gramps.*"

"Don't call me gramps."

"Come on, Earl. You can stay and party with us."

"I don't like people who use the word party like that. You go *to* a party. You don't . . . *party*. I really don't like people who say it like that. It's all wrong."

"So, you don't like me, then, Earl?" she says in a soft, offended voice.

That's not what I meant. She knows that's not what I meant. Why is she doing this to me? Why is she making me say—

"You know. . . ," I say, looking at my great big feet. They are great big feet, bigger, even, than I knew, bigger, even, than they were when I pulled my great big socks over them today. "I like you. You know . . . it."

My vision of my feet is interrupted by Louisa's hand, index finger extended, as she pokes me lightly in the stomach. I have a very flat stomach. It is very flat and hard and I am quite proud of it. I feel myself, stupid, making it harder for when she touches me. I feel myself, stupid, straining to do it.

Her finger makes contact with my abdomen. My

75

rock-hard manly body midriff muscles. She smiles, she notices, which is good because the rest of me is pure jelly.

"I know," she says.

"But I don't like them," I say, pointing past her toward her pack. Right now they have Bobby Norton up in the air, and are passing him around over their heads like a beach ball. Even the girls are doing it.

"You don't like many people, do you, Earl?"

I find my feet again. Still there. Still great big.

"I like you," I remind her in case she forgot.

She takes my hand, and though we have not come to any agreement, I follow her as if she is pulling a wagon.

"I like you, too, Earl Pryor."

It all goes so smoothly in the store, I am out before they have even stopped playing with Bobby.

Wayne comes right up to me. "Big man," he says, arms outstretched.

I clutch the bag to me. "Not until you put him down."

He is down instantly.

"Hey," Bobby says, staggering little semicircles around the parking lot. "What you do that for? Don't stop now."

I hand the bag over to Wayne, who immediately

offers me a can. "You the man," he says.

I turn from him, and Louisa comes up. "Thank you," she says.

"Mmm," I say.

"You stay now," she says.

"I go now," I say.

Nobody will even notice now, when I go, except Louisa. They are filing like a pod of little creatures around to the back of the building, leaving snail trails through the new dusting of snow that replaced the freshly shoveled old dusting of snow. A sharpish whip of wind hurries them along toward the alley-like enclosure that leads on to the shortcut home.

She does not argue with me. She knew all along.

"Thanks," she says.

"Yes," I say.

Louisa backs away politely, at least seeming like it is hard to pull away from me and toward her party. Eventually she is around the corner with a last little wave, and gone.

Bobby stands there, little hands on funny wide hips. He would like to argue with me, I think, but he won't. I'm not a mind-changer much. And he's not likely to stay without me.

"Right then, you big dud," he says. "What do we do?"

If he wasn't Bobby Norton, I'd say he was itching for a fight. His feet are spread wide, his eyes still a little watery and googled from the spinning, and his hands are gripping angrily at his belt.

And I see it there, on his left hand. A big, angry welt, still fresh like out of a grill. Where I had smacked him, hard, for wanting us to stay and play and make new friends where we shouldn't have been making them.

"They had some change," I say, "that I didn't give them back. Can I take you bowling?"

He takes his time, as if he's thinking about it, even drums his little pink fingers on his hip for a few seconds before barking at me, "Fine!"

It wasn't totally a bark, really. More of a yip.

Maybe the best thing about bowling is that you don't have to think about it while you're doing it. That is, if you're any good at the game at all, then your eyes can think for you, and your hands and your feet; then your brain can go on thinking about stuff that really matters. Stuff you really want to think about.

Stuff you really don't want to think about.

I can't stand to see Louisa.

The sounds, too, in the bowling alley, while they

would figure to be a distraction, would figure to be no help at all to the process of thinking, those sounds are great sounds when they blend all up into a wobbly wall. It can be like a crashing surf, or the roar of jet engines at the airport, or any other massive relentless noise that drowns out anything weak and stupid that might otherwise fill your head.

"Jeez, Earl." Bobby doing his version of a shout, over the rumble of the balls and the clack of the pins.

"What?"

"Your feet, man."

"Ya, my feet. Ya?"

"Fourteen."

"I heard the guy, Bob. I know what size the shoes are."

"They weren't that size last time."

I finish tying my laces, and go to the scoring desk to punch in our names.

"I know," I say.

"Jeez," he adds.

She makes me so mad, Louisa does. She makes me so mad. After a while, you can expect most of the world to act a certain way. You can expect the world to judge everything by what they see. You can expect people to not do any better because people, mostly, aren't any better than that. People aren't really better than calling a guy gooch because he's maybe a little big.

Gooch. There's something. Gooch. What does it mean? There's nothing there. There's no meaning there, no real word there. What does it mean? It means nothing. Nothing from nobodies.

It means something. I'm afraid it does.

But it's not that important. I can deal with it, coming from nobodies.

Not coming from Louisa, though. No, she would never call me a name. Never, ever. But from her I expect more. I expect better.

I expect her to see me. I expect her to know me. Because she does know me.

I'm famous, but I'm not well known. I can walk from my house in any direction for fifteen minutes and stand a pretty good chance of getting into a ruck. But I can walk that same radius and not have a prayer of getting into a conversation about anything that means anything to me.

Louisa and I used to have the best conversations. Until they stopped.

"Are you listening to a thing I'm saying?" Bobby wants to know.

"I'm afraid I'm not, Bob. Sorry."

"Well then at least throw the ball, instead of standing there clogging up the lane."

"You don't throw the ball," I say, "you guide it."

"Then guide the ball already."

She knows, Louisa does, that I'm not like other kid kids. She knows better.

Every Saturday, after doing whatever we do, Bobby invites me to come back and have dinner with his family. Every Saturday I say no. I'm not sure why I do this.

"Hey," he says, like some novel madcap idea has just struck him.

"Hey," I say, with somewhat less enthusiasm.

"Good game," he says.

I bowled a 134, a 151, and a 174, apparently. I have never bowled that high before.

"Thanks," I say.

"Hey," he says again, after a short pause.

"Hey," I say.

"How would you like to come over and have dinner with us?" He sounds hopeful, and when he does this, I am filled with a genuine sort of awe. He is ever hopeful, in his way, and I wonder how he manages it. Maybe I should ask him.

"Nah," I say.

"Oh."

"But thanks, though."

"'At's okay."

He scoots up ahead a little now, which is no casual move. It takes him about three strides to every one of mine, for him to show me his back. His little narrow hunched back.

"My moms will have my dinner ready," I say. "She always does. She likes to do that when she can, because with the shifts she works and all. Likes to do the moms thing. You know."

"I know."

She would love to have Bobby over to dinner at our house. I know this because she tells me so. There will be enough food for him because she would give up her place at the table, if I'd only have a friend over one time. She has told me this as well. So I could invite him, without even checking.

We get to the road where we split off to our different directions.

"So I'll see you, then," I say, going my way.

"So," he says, standing, then going. "So I'll see you, then."

I let him go. He lets me go.

I walk half a block toward my home, then I stop.

I don't know why I don't accept his invitations. I don't know why I don't offer him any.

And I don't know why I decide to follow him toward his house, but I know I have to move, because I don't know where he lives.

What do I look like, skulking about outside the Norton house while they try and just be? While they try and just be, and be normal and be decent and be feeding themselves.

A nut job is probably what I look like. What I feel like, though, is a little different from that. I feel like Scrooge being forced by the ghost to peep in at little Tiny Tim and his family eating Christmas dinner.

It's really nice, though. Lord, it's nice. There are four figures, four little Norton figurines, all pretty much Bobby Norton–shaped, and all moving little hands busy across the dining room table. Taking dishes and passing dishes, scooping something onto plates, pouring something, maybe water, maybe gravy, who cares. Bobby is, I think, serving the meal.

Serving. Bobby. I see him enter the room, carrying stuff, leaving stuff, going out and bringing back more. His parents laugh, make comments, poke him, every time he comes. They have white hair. Tall white hair. The last figure is a girl, I think. She looks like Bobby, far as I can tell, but with long dark hair past her shoulders, and glasses, and I believe she is even wearing long white gloves up to her elbows. Bob's the only one who moves about, shuffling in and out like a real professional waiter until he sits down to join them.

They pray, too. Unmistakable, they pray.

Then they go back to saying things. Laughing at things, passing things to each other. Laughing. Eating. Talking.

Lord, look at it.

Lord, thank God I said no.

Good thing I checked.

The town is good and quiet by the time I walk home for my own dinner, and I am good and hungry. It's the only time really, if there ever is a time, when winter won't make you sick down to your feet. The air might still be frigid and clouded, but at least the nighttime has the good grace to shadow it from you. The sky is dark, and black just looks so much better, so much clearer, so much healthier and almost alive than gray ever does. Snowflakes twitch here and there, and when they catch the glint of the street-light now they don't look so horrible, so mean, so total. Put your nose to the air, and if it doesn't freeze right off the front of your face and shatter on the ground, then what you get is the scent of a lot of people of the town doing their bit to fight back against the horror of winter by lighting fires and filling the sky with woodsmoke. I do, after all, love that smell, of the smoke in the air on a rotten winter evening. Even the fact that it's all an illusion, that winter can only seem this okay when it's hiding its mean face up there in the night, even that doesn't kill the feeling entirely when I'm on my way home alone, out of the cold and into my moms's and my Saturday night supper.

When I go past the store, where I left the older kids a few hours before, there is no sign of anything or anybody. Nice. This is nice. For a Saturday with no bones and too many people in it, this is not a bad way to end up, walking through a sharp smoky silence toward something above and beyond.

Until I go around the building, around the back, to cut through my cut through the hedge toward my house.

"Oh," I say, startled by the intrusion. Even if I am the intrusion.

"Hey," Wayne says, backing away from Louisa, who remains leaning, her back to the stiff hedge. "Hey," he says again, overjoyed, apparently, to see me. "Big man. How the hell are you, big man?"

Wayne seems to have appreciated the errand I ran

for him. He smells as if he appreciated it, wobbles as if he appreciated it.

"I'm fine," I say.

"Hi, Earl," Louisa says, and she says it with a dense unusual voice. She continues to hang back, about six feet from me, embedded in that hedge.

"Are you all right?" I ask her.

"'Course she's all right," Wayne says. "Question is, are *you* all right?"

"Like I said," I say again, "I'm fine."

"I know you're fine," he says, "but are you *all right*?"

"I am fine and all right. Louisa?"

"Wayne."

"Big man!" Wayne digs in his pocket again, like before, and fishes out another, yet smaller, knot of crumpled bills.

"No," I say.

"Yes," he says, all chirpy like this is a game we're sharing. It is not. We are not.

"No," I say. "I'm going home for my dinner."

"Okay, bye," Louisa says, rushed and edgy. I don't like the way she sounds. It makes me nervous, the way her voice sounds. It's not like her, not like I know.

Wayne turns and goes to her, right to her, right up close to her.

I can feel, instantly, my palms and my hairline begin to sweat.

"Do that thing," he says to her. He works the money into her hand. "Do that thing you do, where you make him do what you want."

Oh. See. See there, right there, there it is.

See, I know this is bad, as bad as it sounds, because of the way I feel. The way I feel like a kid. Like I feel that my moms is right, and it's better to be a kid. Like I wish I was with her right now, and I could bury my face in her clean bleachy-smelling white nurse's uniform, and do what kids do.

Or go the whole other way, and be big as I am, and get mad and break this Wayne guy in half over my big gooch knee.

Except, really, is he the one? Is he it? Is it him?

"Earl?" Louisa says sadly to me, and that's all she needs to say for me to know.

I am heading out, heading past them, when she says it again. "Earl?" Like my name is a question.

Am I supposed to answer that question for her? Well I couldn't if I tried.

I stop just before the opening in the hedge. I look hard at him, then at her. "Are you all right?" I ask, and I make sure there's a lot of no-fooling in my voice.

She nods.

"The question is. . . ," Wayne butts in.

"Would you like me to walk you home?" I ask.

"No, thank you, Earl."

"No, thank you," Wayne repeats, then leans himself, his whole entire top-to-bottom self, into Louisa, into the firm hedge that holds them in place.

"Thank you," she whispers as I step through the space in the hedge, the opening toward my home.

I wish it was the opening to the center of the earth. I wish it was the opening to deep space, to hell, the way I feel at this second.

"You're welcome," I say.

I really really love the turkey casserole my moms makes me. It's thick with two kinds of cheese including mozzarella, which makes it all sticky and stringy, and there is never too much liquid. She puts in baby peas, which she calls *petit pois* in a big Frenchy accent, and baby carrots, spinach, and capers, and she makes sure that the turkey chunks don't get broken up too small to sink your teeth into.

We sit almost in silence as the two of us bear down on the one helpless dish of the stuff, but it doesn't matter all that much how little talking we do. We're okay with talking or not talking.

I can't get the picture out of my mind. Louisa's face looking right at me, the back of Wayne's head right there alongside her. Looked like the lion sinking into the gazelle's neck.

Was she all right? She was strange. She was not quite right. Should I have left her there? Maybe she wanted me to stay. Maybe she was telling me something with her strangeness, and I was missing it.

I should have known. I shouldn't have left her. She needed me, and I left her. That wasn't right. I should have stayed. I should have known better. I should know these things now.

My dad comes in from work.

My moms gets up from the table.

"Are you finished, Earl?" she asks, hovering over my plate, and my fork, like she's going to snatch them off me. Like this is an Olympic relay, and my fork is the baton.

"Still working on it, Moms. Don't worry about mine, I'll take care of it."

She rubs my cheek with the back of her hand before striding to the sink, turning the taps on to full, powerful power, and washing her own stuff. We have great water pressure, and the spray is getting everywhere, but the pressure is not so great that she could do a proper job of cleaning things in the six seconds she spends there. It'll need to be rewashed when I bring my own stuff over. I don't mind. I've done it before.

Moms deposits her silverware, dish, and glass in the strainer, and she's gone.

Dad sits.

"Melon head," he says.

"Hey, Dad."

"How goes it today?"

"It goes okay."

He pulls out his cigarette pack, taps one up and lights. Instant relaxation comes over his face. He has hit after-work Saturday mode. He works six days, works hard. They both do. He turns his chair around backwards, and leans more into my direction. Smoke comes rolling my way, and he attempts to brush it away, but I stop him by putting my fork out in his direction.

"It's okay," I say. "It doesn't bother me." In fact, the smoke does the same thing for me that it does for him. It relaxes me. 'Cause it's the scent of him. Nobody's dad smells bad.

And I need relaxing. The vision keeps coming back at me. Her face keeps coming back at me. And his head, his body pinning her to that stiff and prickly hedge, her eyes open wide and asking . . .

"What did you do today?" Dad asks, leaning away and pulling on the chair like the reins of a horse.

"Bowled a 174."

He's excited now. He grins, and as he does he grips the cigarette with his teeth, looking like a smoking skeleton head.

"A 174?"

"A 174."

"*I* never even bowled a 174 before."

"Neither did I, before today."

"Who the man?" he says, clapping one time loudly.

"Me the man."

I should have done something. I should not have left her there. A real man would not have left her there. If me the man, then I don't leave her there.

"That's it," Dad says. "Finish eating. We're going bowling."

"Oh . . . Dad, I'm kind of tired. You think we could do it another day?"

"Oh," he says. "Sure we can. Sure. You probably couldn't bowl another 174 today anyway, and I'd just have to whip you like usual. That'd be no fun." He's talking a good game. This doesn't happen. I don't say no to him. I hate to say it. He hates to hear it. But I just can't go, not now.

"Right," I say. "Sorry, Dad."

"Ah, nothing," he says, blowing smoke purposefully at me, which makes me feel better. "Will we watch a movie, then?"

"We will."

He finishes up his cigarette, stubs it out in the rectangle of aluminum foil that had covered the casserole. There are no leftovers to be covered. She doesn't cook for him. She knows, after all these years, exactly how much she and I eat. And she cooks exactly that much.

"Have a bite?" I say, passing him my fork.

"Nah," he says, looking around, as if he's being watched.

I let the fork hang there for a bit, until he takes it and has a couple of bites.

"You didn't tell her, about the school, did you?" he asks as he swallows.

"No, Dad, I didn't."

He nods. Good, he's nodding, good.

"A 174?" he says again.

"Yup." It seems to me now more like a newspaper headline than something I actually did. I barely recall the game.

"Who the man?" he says.

"Me the man, Dad."

Me the man. Right.

I can't shake the vision. Louisa in need. In my mind now, she is there, struggling, her hands outstretched in my direction while I back away, away, away from her.

I carry that vision through the evening. I leave Dad asleep on the couch as I snap off the TV and head to my room. Moms is snoring in her bedroom.

I carry that vision to my room, out of my clothes, into my bed and almost all the way to dreamland with me.

Almost.

I'm pulled back, off the cliff edge of sleep, by the sounds. The voices.

I am not peeping. I am not peeping as I go to the window, I am just curious, like anyone would be. They are too loud, much too loud for this time of the night, which I realize is now officially morning.

I stand, a couple feet back from the window, out of the yellow beam of the streetlight spilling into my room, trying to expose me. I stand just where I can see and not be seen, by her, by him.

I am not peeping. But I don't come away from the window, either.

What is he doing? What is she doing? She should be in the house by now. This is no time for her to be out. She should be in the house by now. It's inhuman freezing cold out there.

And he should be keeping his hands to himself. He keeps on holding her, hugging and tugging and squeezing her, and I don't think she wants him doing that. She doesn't want him doing that, I can tell. How could she want him doing that? He is clumsy and rude, more like a bear pawing at a garbage can than a decent guy being with a girl. He doesn't know how to behave. He should be shown how to behave.

And loud. Shut up, Wayne. Jeez. He keeps laughing, like the whole world needs to see and hear that he's out there with Louisa.

Louisa who should be in the house by now, and not out with this guy who does not know how to act. It's not right. None of this is right.

I take one step closer to the window, and I notice the light catching on my white T-shirt, exploding with light on my white T-shirt, and I jump back, further away now than I was before.

I hear Louisa now, sounds like a short laugh. Must be a small, frightened cry. I stare now, squinting, focusing on Wayne, his small, suspicious little blond head, focusing on his hands, his body. I focus on Louisa, and though it is difficult, though the light is not good and the angle is not good, and my eyes are for some reason hurting and my temples and the areas just behind my eyes are hurting, I see. I see what I see. I have eyes, and I see what I see.

And what I see is not going to go on. No way. Uh-uh, no way. Not this time.

I pull on my clothes in the dark, without taking my eyes off the scene in the street.

Shaltnots

I WAKE UP TO THE SOUND OF GOSPEL CHOIR MUSIC, and that's how I know it's Sunday.

I hate gospel choir music. I like God and Jesus, Mother Mary and the church. I like what they have to say. I like the rules, the order of it all, and I like where I fit into it. It's a system I can go for because I think I understand what they are talking about, and why they are talking about it. I know that it's all about people treating each other right, and that if something like the church isn't there to make sure that happens, then it won't. Because people can't manage to do that consistently without being made to.

I like the Shaltnots. The Shaltnots are the instructions that keep everything from flying apart altogether. If I were God, I'd have Shaltnots all over the place. There should be more of them.

I like heaven and hell, like them very much, in fact. I like to know that some people are going to the one, and the others to the other. Most, to the other. I like to believe that people get what they deserve. I like being in church, I like receiving sacraments like Communion and penance because when I have done it I feel better.

But I have to confess I don't care for the music at all.

And I am not the only one. Shortly—very shortly, like two minutes shortly—after the music goes on, I hear it go off again.

So it begins.

I haven't had enough sleep. Sleep is very important to me, and I spent much too much time last night rolling around and listening to every bit of breeze out there, but I have to get up and out of here because I don't like this.

The music goes back on.

I step out of bed, and into my Sunday pants. They aren't really fancy or anything, the way people used to dress up for church in their Sunday best, but I would say they are my Sunday best. They are black. They have a crease. They look more respectful than anything else I own. I put on a clean button-down white shirt to go with it, big black shoes, and I am on my way.

It is silent in the house, aside from the rising crush of the choir every time the music comes back on, and the even louder ungodly silent noise that hangs in the air after it is shut off again.

Sunday is the only day neither one of them works.

I don't speak to anybody, and I don't even poke my head into the living room as the contest snaps back and forth, in both directions.

I can't even remember which one of them wants it on and which one turns it off.

"Hey, *you!*" she shouts as I reach the slushy sidewalk.

Hey, you. Hey, you, is what I get. I don't think that's called for. I keep walking.

"I called you, Earl."

"You didn't call me Earl. You called me *Hey, you.*"

"I'll call you a lot more than that if you don't stop right now."

"That would be very nice, talking like that on a Sunday."

"Earl, *stop!*" She screams so loud that she must have interrupted breakfast conversations on the other side of town. I stop, feeling the eyes of all worlds on me.

I stand there, waiting, watching, wondering not at all. I have a pretty good idea what she wants to talk about.

"Are you out of your mind?" she barks, slapping me hard on the upper arm.

It stings. I put my hand on the sore spot. I look at it, look at her.

"I don't think I am, no."

"Then how do you explain yourself?"

There's a tough one. There's a really tough one. How do I explain myself? How does anybody explain themselves? I can tell you, I'd really like to hear people explain themselves sometimes, lots of times, anytime. It might as well begin with me, since nobody else is likely to start.

"I did what was right," I explain.

I start walking again, away from her, away from our neighborhood and our neighbors and all the eyes and ears that I know are out there, in there, behind lace curtains like they usually are but still right here, right here, right here.

She catches up, grabs me by the arm but does not stop me. We walk along, not quite together. I go faster, she goes faster, little angry steps keeping up with bigger ones.

"Punching is never a right thing," she says.

"Sometimes it is," I say.

"No, Earl, it isn't. Only morons think that."

"I'm a moron, I guess."

Now I stretch. When I really want to open up my stride, there's no way she can keep up without running.

She starts running as we leave the trees and the same simple squareness of the nice houses on our nice street and turn into Washington Street, where it is bigger, and faster, even on a Sunday morning, where fast cars are on their way to someplace, and where people don't care to stare out their windows at a very pretty girl jogging alongside a lumbering gooch.

"You are not a moron, Earl. That's why it bothers me so much when you act like one."

Here's how things are. Here's what a big baby gooch I really am. I hear her say that to me, about me acting like a moron. But I don't hear it the way a normal person would hear it because what matters, to me, inside, is that she said it bothers her.

Something I did *bothers* Louisa. Something I did *matters* to Louisa.

I feel myself—I'm such a stupid—ready to thank her. I barely get it under control before opening my mouth.

"That's the way you show appreciation, is it?" I say.

It's a few strides before I notice she has stopped keeping up with me. I am about to turn and check on her when I feel it, the big two-handed shove in the middle of my back.

"Ap-pre-ci-*a*-tion?" she snaps, whiplashing my neck at the same time.

I rub my neck, regain my footing, and stand across the sidewalk from her, both of us wide-footed like a couple of gunfighters. A car crunches and clinks past, tire chains chewing up the street and throwing gray-brown muck up everywhere.

I am wounded. I can't believe Louisa actually put her hands on me. "That hurt, you know."

"Just exactly what was I supposed to appreciate, Earl?"

"My saving you last night, from that animal?"

"*Saving?* Is that what that was? You were saving me. So who told you I *needed* saving, Earl? How would you know that? How would somebody like you even begin to be able to figure out something like that?"

Somebody like me.

"How can you even dare call somebody else an animal, the way you go around—?"

"What does that mean, Louisa, somebody like me?

101

Is that like . . . are you trying to make me feel bad? Are you calling me something. . . ?"

She is still standing, facing me, taking me on. But at the same time her face changes, goes soft; her eyes swim around, up, down, away, looking like she's getting away a bit, taking something back a bit.

"I'm not calling you anything, and I'm not trying to hurt your feelings . . ."

I feel half better for half a second. She is hesitating too long.

"Yes I am, Earl, I'm trying to hurt your feelings. Or at least I was. Listen to me. What I'm saying is, you're out of your league here, and you have to stop it. Okay? You don't know what you're doing. You don't understand stuff, and so you can be kind of dangerous—"

Dangerous.

Dangerous. Earl Pryor. What is she talking about? Who is she talking about? She couldn't be talking about me. Not the Earl Pryor I know. Not the Earl Pryor she is *supposed* to know. I feel it building inside of me, like somebody's jammed a hose down my throat and is pumping me full of hot acid until I am about to explode my guts out all over the place.

"I saved you," I blurt in a voice that is mine, but laced through with some little boy's crack and squeak that I haven't heard in a whole year.

Louisa talks softly now, and takes a step toward me. I don't like what I see here. I see in her face, what she thinks she sees in mine. I hate it. I hate what she is going to do now. She's going to be *careful* with me.

"I'll ask you again, Earl: How would you know, if I needed saving?"

I have eyes.

That's a stupid question. I have eyes. She thinks because I'm younger, I don't have proper eyes.

"Why would anyone need to tell me? I have eyes. I can tell. I can figure things out for myself. And that just wasn't right, what was going on out there. With him. What that awful Wayne guy was doing. Just not right at all."

I have eyes. I don't need so much telling. I can see what anybody else can see.

"Earl," Louisa says, and says very kindly, "maybe you wouldn't know *that*, either. What right is, what wrong is. Not for everybody, anyway."

All right now.

So what, that Louisa is sixteen. Even though she is three years older than I am, we look the same. We are, actually, lots the same. She has to respect me for that. She has to not treat me so much like a kid for that. I am not so much like a kid, really, I am in fact not like a regular little kid at all. Louisa has to know that. Most especially Louisa.

"Right and wrong is very clear," I inform her. "Everybody knows it."

"It is nothing of the kind. And the fact that you believe that only proves how confused you are. That was a guy I was with. A guy I like. I don't know what you thought you saw . . ."

"I am not confused."

"But he wasn't doing anything out of line. And he wasn't doing anything I didn't want him—"

"Maybe *you* don't know!" I blurt, as if by being louder I can erase what she's already said. And maybe she doesn't know, anyway. Maybe even though she is sixteen and I am not, maybe she doesn't know everything, and maybe since I am a guy and that bothering guy Wayne is a guy, then maybe I might know something about what he's up to that she might not even know. And maybe in that case she might need a little more help than she thinks, from a good guy, from a big guy, who's her friend and has been her friend longer than he's been practically anything, a guy who wants good things *for* her and nothing *from* her.

"And you have to stop watching me so much. You have to stop paying so much attention to me, Earl.

I'm your *baby-sitter*, for goodness' sake."

She is *not* my baby-sitter. *Not. Not.*

"I wish you wouldn't say that, Louisa," I say, kind of hush-hushy and looking all around, though no one is paying any attention to us.

"Okay," she says. "Okay, I'm not, now. But, you know. You know, after all, what it is with you and me."

What it is, is, she did sit with me a few times. Back then. When things were different, and my parents went out sometimes. And Louisa was close by to sit with me. *With* me. It's a whole 'nother thing. You can sit *with* someone instead of *for* them. And that's how it was.

We sat together, Louisa and me.

And it was the nicest thing, ever.

But we are a million miles away from any of that now. A million worlds and a million lifetimes and I am not a kid and I am certainly not a little kid, and she knows it.

"It wasn't like that," I say.

"It was just like that," she says.

"That's not fair," I say.

"It's as fair as anything else," she says.

It wasn't like baby and sitter, I swear it never was. She knew it and still knows it, and I don't know why she is saying something else now. We talked. We talked stuff. She helped me feel better when I needed to know how to feel better. I helped her when she needed it, too. Nobody's life is perfect, is it? And nobody's parents are perfect, and every, probably, every single one of us could use having somebody come over and hold our hand for an hour at the right time. She held my hand for an hour.

For an hour and six minutes.

"Do you get what I'm saying, Earl? Do you get my meaning?"

My hands were bigger than hers, even back then. Her hands were the softest and warmest things I ever touched, even back then. I felt the heat of her palm already, seconds before she touched me. And then I would do it, take one of my hands and completely wrap up two of hers. It made us both really happy, back when she still had an even harder time being happy than I did.

She knows this. And if she is going to say now that it was like a *baby-sitter* thing . . . well, that's just as wrong as a thing can be, and I should be good and angry.

"You're a lovely boy, Earl. You are a sweet, lovely boy inside."

This, finally, will not do.

I am, actually, so angry now. And the way I am . . . I

am famous for the way I am. We all know the way I am, and it isn't a good way, is it? I just don't know what I might do about this, but everybody everywhere knows by now that, being big Earl Pryor, I'll have to do *something*.

Big ol' Earl. Stupid Earl, the crazy dumb gooch Earl, you don't want to get him angry, because you know he's going to do something about it, when you get him angry, and it's not going to be pretty.

And it isn't.

She goes all wide-eyed at the sight of me now. I am a sight.

"Oh . . . oh, don't. Earl . . ."

I have eyes. I know. I know things. I have eyes.

"Please, Earl. Please, don't. I hate it, I can't stand to see you doing this . . ."

So then you won't see it.

"Earl. Earl Pryor, come back here. *Earl . . .*"

In church, the big one, the original, Catholic one, they let you do anything. As long as you're doing it on the inside. You can have whatever feelings you want, on the inside, as long as your outside is folding its hands and bowing its head and kneeling at the right times and maybe singing if you don't sing so bad that you spoil it for everybody else.

My outside remains quiet. I settle in near the back of the big, near-empty church. It isn't that there's nobody here so much as it's a big place. I figure maybe a hundred people in here, but the thing is, it probably seats a thousand. Maybe fifteen hundred. It's cold here. It's always cold here these days, but what can you do? How do you heat a place that's this big, this stony, and this empty?

But I don't mind. It used to be warmer, but I don't mind. I don't come here to be comfortable, I come here to feel better.

The organ swirls up, and all of us, all hundred, get to our feet as if we are a great big version of one of those creepy old puppet shows, marionettes, I guess, where there is one giant controlling all the little people from above. It's the organist who controls us, though, and he's no giant. I've seen him up close, and he is no giant, and probably wouldn't be considered a giant even to marionettes.

He's a good guy, though, and he can play the hell out of an organ. Thank God there's no choir to poison it.

I have the hymnal, but I don't sing, though I do feel the music in my chest, where you are supposed to feel things. I feel what I am supposed to feel—a kind of bigness, a there's-something-going-on-here sensation, a motion, a movement, a scaredness that's kind of a thrill. What a church should be able to produce, in my view. And what's maybe even better, what maybe I have to confess is just as important to me about church, is that the organ music pushes *out* of my chest the feelings I do not want in there.

That's nice, isn't it? That's good. That's the way a church should work, and that's why I like church. Because it is right. Righteous, I suppose, is what that is.

I can't help looking up over my shoulder, at the organ, at the organist, as the music plays. It's so *big*, up there, like a stampede of musical bison is coming down over us. But I look and I look and there's nothing like that. No hammers of the gods, either. Just one little man playing away on one large gleaming golden-piped organ, up there in the private balcony in the air.

But no choir.

Again, no choir. I wonder, back at home, whether the choir is singing now, or if it's switched off. Or back on again. I wonder who is winning.

The big oak center door creaks open loudly just as the music quiets, and we the congregation sink back into our cold bench seats.

I turn to look. It's hard not to turn and look, even though I know I'm not supposed to. Even though I know it's impolite to the person coming in, who is probably embarrassed enough over being late. Even though it's disrespectful to God who, though He is everywhere, is right now more at the front of the church than He is at the back. In the old days, Moms would have straightened my head into proper altar-facing position. These days, I'm responsible for my own head-straightening. And I catch a look before I do.

It's Bobby Norton. I see him before I turn, and I figure he sees me. Something in me is happy, is thrilled even, at the thought. I like to be by myself at church, in fact I insist on it. I would probably have to admit that one of the reasons I like this church as much as I do is because of the vastness of it. The together aloneness that I share with my fellow worshipers twenty, thirty, and a hundred pews away, and if the place started filling up I would probably have to find myself another place with more space.

But seeing this kid, this Bobby, in this place at this moment, has me a little aflutter. It makes no sense.

I fold my hands tight and wait for him.

He passes me right by. I watch him, walking solemn and small as a first-communioner, as he heads past, up the center aisle, up ten, and twenty, and a hundred pews up. Boldly, late as he is, into the heart of the service.

He must have seen me, he had to see me. Maybe he didn't see me. Why didn't he stop? Why didn't he come and sit with me? I'm his friend, his only friend. I like to be alone, especially at church, but still. Still, I like to be alone, but I don't like to be ignored. He should have sat with me. I don't know much what friends do, what the rules are, but I figure they don't just pass you by.

He didn't see me, that's it. I hope that's it.

It doesn't matter now. It's bothering me, and I'm distracted. I know the moves well enough by now that I can do the right things, kneeling, sitting, standing, shaking hands with the one other remote soul in my pew when it comes time for the sign of peace, mouthing the words to the Apostles' Creed. But I am fretting where I shouldn't be fretting, worrying that Bobby Norton didn't want to sit with me.

Did I do something wrong? I stared in through his window while he ate dinner with his family. That's not what you are supposed to do when you are invited for dinner. You are supposed to say yes and then go inside, not say no, show up anyway, and creep around the grounds like an assassin.

But he doesn't know about that, so . . .

So, have you done anything wrong, if nobody knows about it?

Nuts. Confession. I have to prepare for confession. But I haven't done anything wrong.

I'm lost in this, and more, lost in the Sunday morning tug-of-war going on back at my house. Should that matter, anyway? To me, anyway? What do they do when I'm not there? Is it as quiet when I'm not around? Is it smash-and-crash loud when I'm gone, like they shut up as a favor to me, and then let it all rip in my absence? And does it matter?

What matters is what you see and hear, what you can prove, what lies right in front of you, and the rest is not for you to worry about.

That's what my dad always says.

Louisa thinks I'm an animal. And she thinks I'm a lovely sweet boy. Which do I hate more? Which one of me makes me sicker?

I wonder what they would say, if they went to confession. I wonder what they would tell, all of them. I wonder even if they know what they do?

Communion. Jeez, I'm dead last. I scramble out of my bench and sort of waddle up the center aisle, trying not to run, trying to keep my hands folded properly, but still not be left out.

At least I can be sure he sees me. I am very seeable. The priest—do I know him? Sure I do. And he knows me. You know me, Father. Wait up, one straggler left,

Father, one prodigal left, Father, one big stupid wandering sheep. He's got two old-timers left to serve. He can see me, though. It is an awfully big church. Jeez, this church is so big. One old-timer left. You see me, Father, I'm coming, too.

Now I am standing, big and stupid, three-quarters of the way up to the altar as he turns his back. I am standing with Father's back to me, a mouth empty of the body of Christ and a shroud of blush pulling down over my face and my whole body.

You knew me. You saw me. I know you saw me. How can anybody not see me? So much of the time I want people not to see me, and they can't not see me. Now I want to be seen. See me. You know me, Father, I'm right here.

The church is ten thousand times the size it was before.

I am as big, and as conspicuous, as that Jesus statue on that mountain in Brazil.

I bow my head, which I would have done anyway and for the right reason if I had the chance, and I make for the back of the church, empty.

I know my pew. Could find it with my eyes closed, which is basically what I do. I keep my head bowed, my eyes on the kneeler at my feet, as I sit there and wait for the Mass to be over.

I try mightily to get it back. To regain my Sunday Church feeling before church is over. I need it. I need it. Come back to me.

This wouldn't happen in *my* church. Nobody would ever get embarrassed in my place, if I were in charge.

Thou Shaltnot be embarrassed. That would be one of my Shaltnots. One of my top Shaltnots.

The organ swirls, booms, and squeals. Louisa's face is in my face, but only in my mind. I am not a boy. I am certainly not a lovely boy. I know things. I can see things. I have eyes, and I'm no dope.

Seeing and being seen. Why is it not that simple? Somebody sees me and sees a man. Somebody sees me and sees a boy. Somebody sees me not at all.

And they're all wrong. Like three-card monte, each and every one picks the card and picks the wrong card, lifts the cup and finds no ball underneath, looks at the guy and sees the wrong guy.

Without fail. Every time. Dealer always wins. Who's the dealer?

I am not alone. I startle, like snapping from a shallow and sad dream. A leg is pressed alongside my leg, a shoulder against my arm.

I look up slowly, not expecting the best things, unless it's God. God here finally to share the laugh, to tell me He was just kidding and now when He claps His hands I will wake up and everything will be the way it is supposed to be, and everything will be better. We'll all be the same size and the same age, and the body of Christ will be melting on my grateful tongue.

I turn to the sight of Bobby Norton. He is smiling at me.

He is a very good guy, Bobby Norton.

"Why were you peeping in my window last night?"

Mass has not ended yet. Everybody stands as Father and his altar boys take their position at the front of the congregation, with their backs to the lot of us, and bow to God. We have been given our marching orders. "Go in peace."

"Why were you outside my window? You were invited inside, why would you rather be outside? There was food inside, and people to talk to."

People are filing past now, they are mostly looking over at me. I was a spectacle. I was a scene. I'm one now again. It's like it was once upon a time. I'm being spoken to, like a bad boy, for something I did in church. Only little Bobby is looking up, to scold me, pointing up with his little index finger in my face.

"I'm not a freak show for you, you know," he says. "Were you there for the freak show?"

"There's a laugh," I say.

"No, there is not a laugh. There's not a laugh there at all, thank you very much."

"That's not what I meant. I meant, what a joke that is, me looking at somebody else's freak show."

"So? Why were you peeping?"

How do you say this? Is there any decent way to get through it and sound at all normal?

"I wasn't peeping. I was . . . looking."

Bobby makes a small growl at me. It's funny, because it is so real. He sounds like a very angry dachshund.

"Why were you *looking*?"

Again, how do you begin? Especially when you don't know the answer?

I shrug. He says nothing. I shrug more emphatically. There is a long silence as the organ music flattens out, the church goes calm, and the population completes its split—confessers inside, escapees out in the fresh Sunday air.

"You have it nice," I say.

"Hmmm," he grunts.

"That's really good," I say. "I mean, the way you,

you know, do the serving and waiting on your folks and all."

He is unmoved.

"It is nice, isn't it? You're not like a slave or something."

"They're old," he says.

"And your sister? Was that your sister?"

"She can't," he says, and it is clear that subject is finished.

I wait. Don't know what I'm waiting for. Just as well, since it's not coming.

"Anyway," I say. "It looked nice, is all. Just wanted to say."

"Well. Should have seen it from inside, it looked even nicer, ya gooch."

"Ya freak."

"Shut up."

"You shut up. I'll smack ya."

"So smack me."

"I'll smack ya, Bobby."

"Smack me, for crying out loud."

I'm kind of lost here, because people don't usually tell me to smack them. People are usually afraid of that, see. And Bobby's pretty much afraid of everything, so this is a double shock development.

"You going to confession?" I ask, in the same tone as *I'll smack ya.*

"You gonna confess to peeping in my window?"

"There is no *Thou Shaltnot peep in people's windows*, so, no."

"Then I'm going to tell, when I go in."

"You can't do that. You can't confess for somebody else."

"Well, I'm doing it."

"I'm going to listen, and if you do, I'm going to smack you stupid."

"Well I'm doing it, so go ahead and smack me. Stupid."

Jeez.

"And another thing. If you don't tell what you did, then that's a lie of omission, so as soon as you confessed you're going to be all black-marked all over again."

"Get out of here, Bobby."

He does a double take. I don't know what he was thinking, if he was thinking that the rules had changed somehow, maybe because we were in church, or maybe because I peeped in his window when I shouldn't have. But the rules have not changed.

"Go on," I say, "get out of here."

He gets up without a word. He walks slowly, slowly up that long aisle.

Rules can't change. They can't change, or they were never rules.

I know how long that aisle is. It's a very long aisle.

Father is back out now, out of his cushy-comfy sacristy with the multicolored vestments, the madly shiny purple and green ones, the Lent ones, the Advent ones, the robes and scarves and the long gold staff thing for snuffing out candles and his big red leather throne seat where he would sit like Santa Claus and take visitors forever.

I love all that stuff. Every bit of it. My church would have vestments.

He's gone again, Father is, into his dark and secret cubicle for confession. I used to picture him in there, looking like the United Nations delegates on the news. A headset on him—a gold headset—as he interpreted between you and God, then took it all down as God told him what to make you do for penance. Such a kid, I was then.

My heart is sinking now as I realize this isn't going to work. Church is not going to upend all the things that seem so upside down right now. It's not going to change my parents, and it's not going to change the fact that I have no school to go to in the morning.

And it's not going to make Louisa see what I am and what I am not.

And it was nothing but childish, nothing but a kid's way of thinking, that made me believe church ever could do all that.

I get up, and I make the long walk. I am not prepared to wait any longer than necessary now to get my absolution before he runs out.

I near the front, and I make a big play of sliding hard into Bobby Norton right up there in the front row.

I don't say anything, and neither does he. He even makes like he's not sneaking to sneak a peek in my direction, but I see him.

We leave it at that. That's enough.

When the next person exits the confession box, I am up and in there.

"Bless me, Father, for I have sinned. It has been—"

"Perhaps next time," he says in his dark whisper, "you should sit closer to the altar, where you can be part of my Mass."

My mouth is just hanging there open. Then it feels to me like he can see even that. I shut it.

They are not supposed to know you. They are not supposed to know you.

I stand quickly and rap my head on the top of the doorway, but step straight out just the same.

I pass Bobby on the way. "That was quick," he says. "You didn't tell anything . . ."

I tap his arm on my way by. "You can finish up for me," I say.

They are not supposed to know you. That's not right.

They are not supposed to know you. Why can't anybody get it right?

The rest of my Sunday will be spent in Pryor Church. Maybe I'll confess there, if I still feel like it. Maybe somebody there will be willing to listen.

In my church you'll just have to say *sorry*, and then penance will be done. Just sorry, and bye.

Or not sorry, even. Just, oh well.

Lamb Chops
and Sweet Potatoes

IT'S MOMS WHO WAKES ME UP. DAD IS DAY-SHIFTING at work, so she'll be around the house all day. She'd never leave it, I think, if she didn't have to. She smells like laundry as she leans over me—detergent, bleach, and spring meadow fabric softener. I breathe it in with my eyes closed as she gives me the alert.

"Time for school, Earl."

Right. Oh, right. True, it is time for school, for somebody, for lots of somebodies. But not for me.

"Right, Moms," I say, like I always say.

She just can't know. I don't care much what happens to me. In fact, nothing much ever would happen to me. Except inside. Moms can rough me up something serious on the inside. With a wet droopy eye, a bitten lip, a small mouse-squeak of a cry that can come out of her at the worst of times. But that is the worst. She'll never so much as raise her voice to me these days, much less her hand. No, she wouldn't be hard on me.

It's the rest of it. What all else would go on in this house, if she found out I was barred from school, on account of my hands. I couldn't bear to cause all that I would cause. For that reason, I couldn't tell her, ever. For that reason, I have to carry on with this. Even though yes, I know, it's a lie of omission.

"Right, Moms," I say. "I'm getting up and out."

Up and out where?

Up from the bed, sure. I can do that. Out of my bedroom. There we go. Beyond that . . .

She is awfully chatty at breakfast. I don't like to play favorites, but I sure wish this was Dad's morning.

"So, how is everything going?" she asks.

"Everything's going well," I say. I cram a whole piece of toast into my mouth.

"Oh, my, Earl, don't eat like that, there's plenty, take your time. How about lunch? You look thin to me. Am I making you enough? Maybe you should get the cafeteria lunch, have something hot for a change at lunchtime. Maybe that would be better, huh? You don't have to worry about hurting my—"

I take my next piece of toast, and I quickly slip it into her mouth, mid-sentence.

Her eyes go all wide, then all squinted. She's only outraged for a second before smiling and biting down on the toast.

"Your lunches are fine, Moms. Perfect. The best. I wouldn't want anything else, so don't worry about that. And I'm not getting skinny."

"You need to shave," she says, reaching out across our teacups, our juice glasses, cereal bowls, and bread plates. She always sets a proper table, Moms does, even if she's not eating much. She strokes my chin, and I can hear it as if she's sweeping the sidewalk.

"Ya," I say. "It's been a while. I'll get to it."

"Oh," she says. "Well, I don't think you can get to it now, or you'll be late for school. I'm afraid you have to go."

It seems a simple enough thing to say under the circumstances. It is getting near schooltime, for the schoolgoing population. But it doesn't sound quite right. Not the first time.

And not the second time.

"I'm afraid you have to go," she repeats, as she takes the plates, some of them perfectly clean plates, to the sink for washing.

I'm left sitting there, not quite knowing what to

do. She sounds so sad. My moms. My strong moms, who is a nurse, a boss nurse, who spends her longest hours helping folks who really need it to get through what they need to get through. Now she is gone all scary blue over the small untrue fact that I have to be leaving for school.

I could just tell her that as a matter of fact I have the day off. And, come to think of it, several more. We could hang out. I could lift her spirits, and she could fatten me up.

I could tell her the story of how I used this big hand like Thor's hammer to show one smartface punk the error of his ways, and how the school's administration failed to see the light on the subject. Again.

Well, no. I couldn't, could I?

I get up from the table. Quietly I walk up to her, stand right behind her where she's needlessly scrubbing away at those poor dishes.

"You know what I'm thinking about?" I say, leaning down so I'm half-muffled, talking into her shoulder blade. But she can understand me. "I'm thinking about hearty soups. Like potato-corn chowder."

"Like summer-squash-and-red-pepper soup."

"Exactly," I say, and the thought actually does fill me, fills my stomach with something way different from the usual food reactions.

"Think we could maybe have that tonight? Maybe a hearty soup night? It's been a while. Maybe I'll even shave for the occasion."

I can feel it, the way the flesh of her cheek puffs out with her smile, but then deflates again.

"I'll have left for work when you get home. But the soup will be waiting."

Right. She won't be here.

I kiss her on the cheek, head for the back door. There is a little chime thing that jingles over that back kitchen door when you open it, and as the chime goes, Moms spins and calls my name.

"Earl," she says, a tiny, trembly screech in there, something that has partly already hidden away again by the time I turn to look at her.

I stand in the doorway. She stands, soaking-wet soapy hands on her hips. "Love your moms?" she asks faintly.

"Love my moms."

Love my moms. Love my moms like mad. Was a time, everybody loved my moms. And Moms loved everybody.

Everybody was food in this house. Lamb chop. Dumpling. Honey pie. Sweet potato.

"My sweetie sweet potato."

"There you are, lamb chop. You're late."

"Sorry, sugar. Work was busy. Where's that little sprout?"

"Here I am, Daddy Donuts," I said, bombing like a rocket into the house, into the room, into his arms.

"Make my eyes pop out," he insisted.

"Go on, Earl," she encouraged me, "make them pop out. I'll catch them."

"Go on, my little man," he said. "Go on. You can do it. I think I feel one popping loose. Show me what you got."

I squeezed, and I squeezed, and I squeezed, and I squeezed, until I thought my own eyes would pop out and my own teeth would snap from the gritting and grinning.

And all I could see were Moms's eyes, and Moms's teeth, and boy oh boy they were fit to pop out in every which direction.

"This is one strong boy, sweet potato," Dad grunted to Moms.

"Yes, that's a mighty boy we made there. Powerful boy."

"What are we going to do with this boy, Moms?"

"What *can* we do with him, big and strong as he is?"

The whole time now, the whole time, he never let me go, never loosened up, and neither did I. Took a lot of strength to keep it up. But it took no effort.

I think, for a moment, for the craziness of it, I was near to passing out, the air seeping out of my squished lungs. Until Moms was around the back of me, and buzzing in my ear.

"The only thing we can do with him, I guess . . ."

I felt her hands slide up my sides, under my arms.

"Love him. We just better love him, Dad."

"I suppose we just better, then."

And there, they went and loved me. Moms held me under the arms, Dad took my feet, and they went on and had the biggest human stretch fight of all time. It went on forever. It didn't go on long enough.

He couldn't stop laughing, she couldn't stop laughing, I couldn't stop laughing, as they dragged in their opposite directions and stretched me an extra inch, six inches, fifty inches, and stretching on into endless time, straight through to the right now, on into I don't know when.

Right now I'm following Louisa.

"Get out of here, Earl, I mean it."

"What, get out? We're outside. You can't kick me out of outside."

"Go *away*. You're only going to make trouble for everybody. Go to school. See what I'm doing? I'm going to school. Now you do the same."

"I'll go to school with you."

"Can't do that."

"Sure I can."

"No, because I go to high school, and you go to junior high. See, Earl, they are different schools. Whole different schools. For *whole different people*. Do you get it, Earl?"

"No. I don't get it."

"Get it. High school is for big people and junior high is for little people—and I'm not talking about height. Go to school, Earl."

"Ya, well, I'm not going to school."

Finally, she stops. I could have caught up to her anyway, but catching her would not have been the right thing to do. That wouldn't have seemed very nice, like I was doing something wrong, chasing. But now that she has stopped to let me catch up, that's different. That's all right. That's an invitation, breaking nobody's rules.

"Why are you not going to school, Earl? You sick? You look pretty healthy to me."

"I'm healthy, thanks. It's just . . . I'm not allowed, this week."

I haven't finished explaining before her shoulders droop, her head falls, and she starts rubbing her temples with her fingertips. I reach to her, putting both of my hands over hers, and bending my knees deeply to try and get a look in at her face.

"Louisa, are you all right?"

She angrily pushes my hands away. "What is going to happen with you, Earl? What are you going to do with yourself? You know, someday you're not going to be able to solve things just by being the biggest kid in the schoolyard. Are you aware—"

"I don't do that."

"Yes, you do. You keep punching everything that makes you mad. Or scared. Or confused. Just being the biggest—"

"Stop it," I say, and I feel it all, the same old bad something, bubbling up. I hate that she thinks this. She should not think this. She should know me better. She knows I'm more than just big.

"I'm *not* just the biggest," I say. "There's a lot more to it, you know."

She stares at me, red and blown up as if she is going to really let loose.

She just exhales. Then inhales. Then speaks slowly.

"Why should I care?"

"What?"

"I said, why should I even care?" She looks at her watch. Then back at me. "I have to get to school, no matter what you have to do, so I'm going to be brief. My point is, I don't see why I should care. Why I should care whether you go to school or not. Why I should care if you go on two-fisting your way through your little life until your time comes—and it's coming soon, you betcha—when somebody caves in your big stupid head and I have to find you in a puddle of mush on the sidewalk in front of my house. I don't see, Earl, why I should spend my time talking to you in the middle of the night because you don't approve of my date. I don't see why I should care that you don't seem aware that there is a million-mile gulf between who you are and who I am. And I don't see why I should care enough to let you stand here this morning and make me late for school.

"Well you know what? The answer is, there *is* no reason I should care."

I am just standing there. Like a dummy. Like a great big giant stupid dummy, staring at her, like a concrete statue of a giant stupid dummy, not showing her anything of the torn and shredded bits of my insides.

I don't know what I'll do if I have to stand here like this another second. I don't get to find out anyway.

Practically leaping off the sidewalk, she blasts me in the chest with a shove that staggers me back, my hand on my chest, catching my breath. I'm starting to wonder which of the two of us is the tough nut.

"There's no *reason* I should care! So why do I? Why is that? Why do I care? This is not fair, Earl. It's not *right*. I don't want to care about you, and I shouldn't have to. I can't stand that I *do*."

She turns away from me, and pounds her way toward her big people's school, away from me. Angrily, away from me.

I'm frozen again. Watching her. Absorbing it.

So thrilled, I'm breathless.

You heard it. That was it. That's what love sounds like. I knew it was in there. I always knew. I knew it had to come out sometime.

There is hope. There is hope everywhere now.

Pryor Church has become my place of refuge. And good thing, too, because otherwise where am I going to go, what am I going to do with myself?

I get nicely lost in my days here, rummaging through the remains of the old life, the life of the church as it was, and the life of the old pastor who ran it. I am always free here. Free to be alone. Free to do what I please, or do nothing at all, which is rare.

Because from the first moment I stepped into the place, there always seemed to be something to pay attention to, something that made me want to follow and understand, something I could swear wasn't there before.

And there are never any real live people cluttering up the place, to get in the way of my doing it. Never. Not once in the whole year I've been coming. I am not sharing this with anyone, and maybe that's the best thing about it.

All right. I have to confess. It does seem that I am developing a little problem with actual people.

But so what. I'm all right.

This is my church. I love my church and I love my moms and I love my dad. Nobody can ask for more than that.

Maybe my church is a kind of gift, even, meant for me personally—or at least somebody a lot like me. For starters, it is no ordinary house of God. It is a house of gods. There is something for everybody here, everybody from everywhere, as if the pastor was afraid he was going to lose out if he didn't cover all the bases of all the religions and then some. There are pictures on the wall, high above the altar, of Jesus, and Buddha, and a whole lot of bearded guys I can't identify, of some holy-looking women with veils, of elephants and unicorns and Bob Marley and some kind of alien with a spiky scaled head, spectacles, and a smile with spaces between rounded teeth like somebody from *The Simpsons*. There's one that I swear looks just like Cap'n Crunch, and one right near him looks like Mrs. Butterworth the syrup lady.

There is nothing like a boss up there, on the altar, nothing like a focus, so that if you were preaching away you would have a feeling less like your God was looking over your shoulder, and so God help you if you messed up, and more like, All right, I got the whole team behind me.

Which is nice. Which is really nice, because *I* never would have thought of anything like it even though it suits me right down to the ground.

And because I am up here, up here a lot. Preaching.

Don't know what it is. Don't know what I figure to accomplish up here, talking away at nobody except the occasional cat who only comes by to warm up a bit or drop off a dead bird for me like an offering before padding off and out a window again.

But I love it. Preaching to nobody, with the team behind me lending a hand. Shutting up, but helping out.

What more could a guy ask for. This might be happiness, I suppose. You think?

I'm very good at it, the preaching. Not that there's anyone to tell me different.

"Hey!"

I nearly dive headlong off the podium. The voice, a thin, screechy little yelp, snaps around the walls of the place for what seems like ten minutes after the original outburst. It is the most foreign sound in the world, after a year of holding the floor all to myself.

I feel myself shrinking a bit behind the lectern. Which must look fairly stupid. I can see nobody, but I don't figure it's God speaking to me because God's voice would be deeper.

"Come out," I call. My voice sounds like I'm five. Like I'm five, and trying to sound big. "Where are you? Get out of my church."

"No."

My body, not to mention my mind, is very confused. I feel my fists at my sides, banging and banging on my thighs. My heart is triple-beating. It's just a voice, just a human voice, but because it is here, it sounds so completely not right.

"Step out and stop hiding," I call, some of the old hard guy coming back now. This is my church, after all. What is he doing in *my* church? "Show yourself," I demand again, louder. I kind of like the way I'm sounding.

"No," he says.

"Stop saying no to me," I shout.

"Stop telling me what to do." He is also getting louder.

I am all puffed up now, to my biggest self, hulking way above everything and everyone who dares to be lurking in my church.

"You could be a priest, you know that? You might have a calling."

"Shut up. What would you know."

"Plenty. Been listening to you rattle on for an hour now."

My whole body shivers at once. I picture it. I hear it. I shudder again. I can't stand the thought.

"You're lying."

There is a silence now. Finally. A good, long, chunky warm silence like the kind that is supposed to exist here in my church except when I am doing the talking.

The mind plays tricks. It could have been nothing. It could have been my echo. I was thinking out loud. I do that sometimes. I sort of lose track. You can lose track, out here, alone with yourself. Voices in the head. I am working up a sweat, trying to make any and all these things be true, to give me back my solitude and my private church.

Silence. I love the silence. God, I love the silence. Funny how quickly you can forget, when you don't have it, how much you need it.

"Louisa can't love you the way you want," he says, gashing the silence, slaying it for good and forever.

I have no words. I have no words for this, but I sure do have fists. My body wants to answer him where my mind and mouth cannot. I bang the podium, and it rings like a drum.

"Listen," I bark, then give him nothing to listen to.

"If you are going to pray for things like that, then you should pray to the right saint. Saint Jude is the patron saint of lost causes. That would be Louisa."

Now all I can do is grip the edges of the podium. I can hear the old wood crackling, in the midst of all the other silence. He has gone quiet again, and the church and the world are again nestled into the complete stillness of the snow-doused woods.

I look all around, cock an ear here and there like an owl trying to pick up on him.

"How. . . ," I begin.

"Been following you since you left the house this morning."

"You little . . . you little freak. You've been sneaking and spying on me all this—"

"Why not? You did it to me."

"You should be in school, idiot."

"Uh-uh. Not without you there. Forget it. Where you go, I go."

That tears it. I hop right down off the altar, head for the sound of his demented little voice. I find him, lying flat facedown on the freezing cold floor underneath the third pew from the back.

"I'm going to break your head, you know that?"

"Don't break my head, Earl," he says, turning his face halfway toward me, holding his body tight to the floor, looking like a mole.

I reach in under there and, though he is struggling, it is barely any effort at all to remove him from his burrow. I carry him, to the door, to the outside world, and point him in the direction of the town.

"You can't be here," I say flatly.

"Let me stay," he says. "Come on, Earl."

"Go away," I say, pointing in case he missed the hint. "You've messed everything up. You had no right. Get out, before you make it worse. Forget you heard anything if you heard anything. Forget you know where this place is. It's *mine*."

Bobby Norton stands there for a minute, shivering.

"Go to school," I say.

He answers as if I have just thrown him off a cliff.

"Okay, Earl. I will. I hope you are happy."

"I hope I'm happy, too," I say, "but I'm not holding my breath."

He starts tromping off, through the freezing sludge that reaches way higher up on his legs than it does on my body, or even a regular body. I stomp loudly and angrily back in, and slam the door with more force still.

Then I slink to the window and peek at him, fighting his way along. Working his heart out. Thrashing and flailing and taking so long to go so short a distance of the longer distance.

Not my problem. My problem is that I have been upturned—my peace, my place, my sanctuary, has been shattered. My problem is that I can't relax now. I spend the next hour picking the place apart, looking for whoever else. He's not in the pews, he's not in the pastor's room at the back, and he's not in the storage room in the cellar. I look behind metal shelves and under rotting tiles and even up in the nooks of the shaky beamed ceiling where you only go if you are a bat or a guy with a death wish. As a last resort, I even venture into the tiny cubicle bathroom, where I do not even go when I need to go, because it is so vile the devil himself would not chase your soul into there.

But he is nowhere. Nobody is.

I have come up and out the bulkhead door looking for nobody, and find myself standing in the middle of a thick and downy snowfall, all around me, all over me.

It is always snowing. God, it is always snowing now. Sometimes it's lighter snowfall, sometimes heavy, sometimes drier, sometimes icy. But never does it stop, as far as I can tell. There is always crunching underfoot. Always.

I look at the tracks, at the tiny, draggy Bobby Norton tracks. Signs of the struggle. I look off, and can no longer see the actual Bob, but I know he's still out there thrashing, making his way to the school like I told him.

It is cold, but probably no colder outside the church than it is inside. I need to go inside.

It is not a lost cause. I will not pray to Saint Jude.

I will do the Stations of the Cross. My church has the nicest Stations of the Cross panels around the walls.

Jesus falls for the second time, that's where I left off. I often leave off there. That's a tough one, Jesus falls for the second time.

I have to add that to the Shaltnots of my church. Thou Shaltnot fall down. It is so awful to see, when someone falls down.

‡‡‡

By the time school is letting out, I am there. Not there, exactly, but half a block away, down the street from the gate where we exit. I can see Bobby Norton. I can see he has company, and attention, like he doesn't normally have. I see his books hit the ground. He picks them up. Ten feet later, they fall again. He picks them up. This goes on, and on, all the way up the street. They knock them down, he picks them up. He has no friends, my Bobby. All he has is me.

I know who they are. I know these numbers.

On it goes, and on it goes, up the street where I would normally be walking along with him.

Whatsoever you do, to the least of my brothers.

He certainly is that.

Coming my way. Come along. Come to me.

Night Sweats

I THINK I CAN REMEMBER THE LAST TIME THEY TRIED.

They did it for me. They do everything for me.

We were going out on my moms's birthday. No, it was the day after her birthday because she was sick on her actual birthday and so all she asked for from anybody was silence.

We gave her silence for her birthday, then we gave her apple picking for the day after.

Dad drove the big Ford up Route 93 into New Hampshire on one of my favorite kind of cool white-sky October days that make me forget how soon and how completely the cool and white becomes cold, bitter, and bruised. Then we have the winter, which around here shows up almost as soon as the apples hit the ground, and stays forever.

Moms likes those autumn days, too, and she has always loved the whole apple-picking thing to pieces. Every stage, every scrap, from the hours in the car, to the choosing and plucking just the right Macs for eating and Cortlands for cooking applesauce and apple-walnut tarts and parsnip-and-apple soup, to inhaling the vapors of the day's work all the way home with one bag of apples on the seat beside her and sacks and sacks more bouncing around in the trunk.

Dad never liked it much, though. He did it for her, and for me, and he did it happily enough. Then he did it for her, and for me, and he did it with a kind of joke grouchiness. Then he did it with the real kind of grouchiness.

Then he did it, that last time, for reasons that were not really clear, did it, I guess because he had always done it, did it because it was Moms's birthday and it was clear October weather and probably it would have taken more effort to stop this thing we did than to keep it going.

"Would you slow down, please?" Moms said just as we passed the BIENVENUE/WELCOME TO NEW HAMPSHIRE sign. "You are going awfully fast."

"It's not awful," he said. "It's the way I drive."

"No it isn't. You'll get a speeding ticket."

"I have never gotten a speeding ticket in my life."

"Yes you have. You got that one in Florida, not long before we were married."

He paused, as if he were trying to remember. But I think he was really just trying to come up with a remark.

"That was before we were married. Everything slowed down after that." He let out a small chuckle. He would do that sometimes, say something that maybe was kind of funny but maybe was also a little nasty at the same time. But whenever he would, he would let out a little laugh right after, trying to make it back into a joke, the laugh chasing out after the words to try and drag them back or remove the stinger before it was too late.

Moms sighed. "Yes," she said. She cranked her window a couple of inches, lifted her nose lightly toward the air. "Yes," she said again.

Same place every year. Mabley's U-Pick-Em. They always had a great selection of varieties of fruit, even though we stuck strictly to the Macintosh and Cortland. And Moms always claimed that she had researched every pick-your-own farm in New England and Mabley's offered the best value-for-money deal. Moms has always used the term value-for-money more than anyone I know. It means a great deal to her.

"Have you factored in the gas that we have to put into the big Ford?" Dad asked her this day, this last birthday.

"What?"

"The gas. It's a thirsty car, and when you work in the price of the tank of gas it takes us to go round trip . . . and then there's the going out to eat . . . I bet if you worked it all out against the price of apples from Stop'n'Shop, which, this time of the year in this part of the country, they're practically giving away, jeez, y'know, it's like we are paying *them* for the privilege of letting us do the work harvesting the fruit for them . . ."

We had just stepped out of the car, onto the stony plot of ground that Mabley's called their parking lot. Moms and I were on our side of the car, staring over the top of the big Ford at Dad over on his.

What was he doing? He was probably right—he never did shoot off his mouth if he wasn't pretty sure what he was talking about—but so what? If this was true, then it was always true. And unless the distance to New Hampshire had suddenly grown or a tank of gas was suddenly lots more than it ever was or lunch at a diner that used to be a train car and had no heat but served an excellent hash was suddenly beyond his means, then there wasn't any reason to point this out, was there?

"We don't have to go to lunch," Moms said quietly, then turned and headed for the trees.

I stood there, staring at him across the car's roof. If I needed to count the times I have gotten truly mad at my dad, I could use a lot fewer fingers than I've got. He's my dad.

"What are you doing?" I snarled.

He looked quickly away from me, down, and made busy with locking the car door with his fat jangly tangle of keys.

"Dad?" I said, more strongly still. "That's not right, Dad, and you know it. What are you doing? Dad?"

When finally, ages later, he finally hauled his big heavy head back up to face me, he didn't quite look like my dad. He didn't look like the straight and sure, right and certain guy with both feet planted wide and firm, wagging a finger at the world or whatever part of it was not up to scratch. Which was most of it.

He looked as if he was the one with the hurt feelings. He looked like he was the one who had been insulted, or scolded, or told that something important and special was actually neither one. His eyes were red, and his lips were pulled tight together in a not-quite-real way.

"I'm sorry," he said, looking straight into me.

"What are you telling *me* for?" I gestured wildly off into the distance, where Moms had already picked up the strong white plastic-coated shopping bags they give you for the apples. She was headed for the Cortlands, thinking already pies.

"Right," he said. "Listen, I'm sorry, Earl."

There he did it again, and all the while looking at me with eyes rounder and wetter and younger and less focused than his eyes ever were. He made me so mad. He made me crazy. He made me want to go over there and give him a wake-up slap. He made me want to make him feel better.

"Grrrr" was all I could manage to say before I slapped the roof of the big Ford with an open palm and stomped off for the orchard.

My best trick—not that I have many—was always to find a medium-low branch, pull it down to my level, and take a great mother bite out of an apple and leave it there on the tree. It was a tradition.

I wondered if it would keep growing, whether it could heal and scab over, whether it could repair itself since it was still attached to the tree or if the show was over for that apple then and there.

But I did it for a laugh more than for science. I was doing that, for Moms's amusement and for the sake of tradition, when Dad descended the small hill from the parking lot.

"I'm sorry," Dad said.

There were about ten other people picking fruit in our general area. From the way he had positioned himself at the foot of the hill, not quite in the orchard yet, and the tone and casting of his voice, he could possibly have been talking to any one of them.

Moms chose to believe he was talking to somebody else. She went on picking.

He took a few steps closer, talked a little more directly.

"You know, um, you make the best pies," he said. He then, with a great jerking motion, snapped his bag open with a loud bang. He came right up to our spot, jumped a bit to grab a branch.

He pulled it down to where Moms could reach a clutch of bumpy, bright red, exploding pepper-shaped apples.

She stared at the apples. She stared at him. He stared at her.

I could have reached that branch without even jumping, I thought.

"I'm sorry," he said again as the apples hung there

doing nothing much for anybody.

I got a shiver then, a terrible awful shiver and a squiggle in my stomach like I had swallowed something live, like I had eaten an apple many months too soon, green and packed with worms.

"I know you are," she said. "We're both sorry. Everybody's sorry."

I knew the difference. There are different kinds of sorrys, maybe hundreds, maybe thousands of them that I don't know about yet. But I knew already there was more than one, and a person could say they were sorry truthfully and it could mean "I feel bad about what I just did and I take it back." Or it could be like when a doctor or policeman on TV tells some poor innocent sap that he's sorry, they did all they could do, but it just wasn't enough. He's sorry. Terribly sorry.

I had a lot of time, during the picking of the apples, to think about the variety of sorrys and the differences between them. I had a lot of time, during the long ride home down out of New Hampshire, during the long silent ride home in the big quiet Ford, with no food in my belly from any great cold oily diner. With nothing inside there but apples and apples and apples that I buzzed through like a beaver goes at trees.

⚇⚇⚇

I wake up with the night sweats, like I sometimes do. I keep my spare T-shirt hanging on the chair beside my bed now, for all the times I wake up, soaked and chilled and chattering like I have been sweating through a marathon for three or four hours without knowing it.

And I wake up to a fly buzzing around my head, sounding like an airplane. He is so loud, I have to turn the light on to get a look at him, because I just have to meet this guy. I've heard him, I know his sound from visits and visits in the nights before, but I have not yet laid eyes on him.

He looks like a furry black grape with wings. He is not in any way disturbed by me sitting up, then standing, then walking around following to get the best possible view of him. Because he is a specimen. And a marvel, since I can't even remember the last time I saw a fly. It is winter. It is deep and frozen and petrified winter here, now, like it always is. He is a very slow fly. I get great looks at him when he lands and waddles around and rubs his little hands together and makes that horrible racket he makes. He's almost cute. I wonder how he survives, being so slow.

I turn off the light again, and drag my chair over to

the window where I turn it around backwards and stare out at the dry icy snow tumbling down past the streetlight. It's snowing. It's always snowing.

I can almost feel good about it, watching it from my room, my window, from inside my fresh and warm triple-thick oversize T-shirt. I hear the fly buzzing, louder now, like he's got a microphone. He's over behind me, around where I dropped my sweaty shirt. I bet that's why he comes. I bet he is attracted by my raunchy sweat. That would make sense.

In fact, I'm sure of it now. He is only here on the nights when I wake up sweating.

The snow is sneaky snow. I'm the only one who knows about it, because I am watching it. It's the type, that very dry, crystal, light stuff that falls and falls during the night, but because it is so thin it is not obvious the next day whether or not there is actually any more ground cover than there was yesterday.

But there is. There is always more. It just keeps coming and coming.

I don't know how long I am watching the snow fall, in its same monotonous pattern, past the light, past the window, onto the ground without a sound, past the light, past the window, onto the ground without a sound, past the light, past the window, onto the ground without a sound.

They say that no two snowflakes are alike. I say that's nonsense. They are all alike.

I don't know how long it is, but I know that finally I am tired again. I know that I need to sleep, and when I don't sleep things are just even worse. I have to sleep.

I sit on the side of the bed, and as soon as I do, the fly starts up. Was he sleeping in my bed? Did I wake *him* up for once and now he's upset?

He won't stop. I have to sleep. When I don't sleep it's a lot worse. He won't stop.

I sit upright, switch on the light. As if it's his turn, his curiosity we now have to satisfy, he is hovering right in front of my face, doing that weird little fly side-to-side pattern they do, but doing it slower than a normal fly would.

We stare at each other. I'm looking at him, he's looking at me. I have to squint more now, have to blink to try and focus because like I said, I'm really really tired now and my eyes are like they have a coating of Vaseline over them. Does he have lots of eyes there? Or is that spiders?

He is louder, and then he is louder. He is an airplane again. Now he's a helicopter.

Of all the places he could be, even in this very

house, why does he need to be here, with me, when I couldn't sleep but now I can, and I really, really *have* to. Can't I have just that? Can't I?

He is a low-flying helicopter now.

I slap him. My hands are like big flat flyswatters anyway, and I reach right out there, swat, catch him like a handball, and smack him off the wall. Off two walls, actually, as he hits the corner, caroms off the one wall, then the other.

I hear it, both times. A little *puh-puh* sequence before he drops to the floor behind my night table.

I'm pretty sure I've killed him because there is a little stuff left on the wall.

Spring Meadow

THERE IS NO FLY ON MY FLOOR, BEHIND MY NIGHT table. I hit the floor, crawl to the spot. Nothing. Look under the night table. Nothing. I feel my way back up the wall, checking, examining for the spot, the spots, the smack and the leakage where he should have hit the wall, where he *never* should have hit the wall.

There is no mark.

I am sorry. I am sorry.

Maybe he was never there. Maybe I never woke up. My stinking rotten sweated-up shirt is there on the floor. Maybe it was an illusion.

Or maybe he recovered. I hope he recovered. He was a big strapping thing, a huge super muscle-fly, so maybe he just got his bell rung, the way boxers do.

Maybe he just shook his hairy head, got his faculties back, and got outta here.

I am sorry. I hope I see him again.

Nobody is home. Nobody wakes me up. Why is nobody home? Why did nobody wake me up for school, even though I don't have any school?

I walk through the house, down the hall, through the bare dining room, into the kitchen where nobody is waiting, nobody is cooking, no food is sitting.

I stand there staring at the empty table, at the cold stove.

And I feel like I'm standing on the moon.

"Oh, hi," she says, sweeping in from the backyard with a *brrrr* and a whoosh of cold air behind her. "Oh, I was just going to wake you," she says.

"Where were you, Moms?" I ask.

"Just hanging the laundry. I love it when I can hang the laundry, when it's finally dry enough to start hanging in the open air again. Thank God this awful winter is finally breaking."

I stare at her, hoping she is pulling my leg, certain she is not. She smiles an angel's smile.

"It's a million degrees below zero, Moms."

"It is nothing of the kind. You so exaggerate."

"Moms, the clothes are going to break. Take them in."

"I won't. Don't be silly. Will I make you some breakfast?"

"I ate."

"You didn't. What did you eat?"

"I ate. I have to get to school, Moms."

I make my way out, grabbing my jacket off one of the hooks right beside the back door.

"Take your gloves," she says as I open the door.

She knows I never wear gloves.

"It's springtime, remember?" I say, and shut the door behind me.

It is as if I walk into a concrete wall.

The laundry. God, the laundry. Stupid little thing, meaningless little thing, nobody's fault, nobody's doing. It's just the laundry, on the line, in the dead of dead-soul winter.

It's the only thing now. The only complete thing, stupid that it is, useless that it is, meaningless that it is.

Her clothes, his clothes, my clothes, three stupids' clothes, all in a row. Together. Hers, mine, his. Always how it was, still how it is. Force of habit. She is still a creature of habit, like I am. Like he is.

The only place, only way, we are still hung correctly.

I walk up to it, put my nose to a flannel shirt of my dad's. Fabric softener. Spring meadow. It could kill me, this scent, this feeling, right here.

Stupid, I know. Meaningless, I know. Who cares, I know.

Anyway, a stiff wicked wind is coming along anytime now, to snap those frozen clothes into a million smithereens.

Winter over. What is she thinking? It is so sad, to think of what she's thinking.

Granted, the sun is out.

But that just makes it worse. It throws the spotlight on the pukey brown slush that lines the curbs and banks up along either side of every shoveled driveway. And it hurts your eyes, gives you headaches, makes you sick, when the sun hits on those remaining spots where the snow remains white for more than an hour after it hits the ground.

It's all snows, all kinds, all the time. It's soft on top, then slushy just beneath, then crunchy where it is old and established and refusing to give up. The crunchy part is the killer. The other stuff gets in your socks, but the crunch, crunch, crunch that won't let you take a step without talking to you, that's the killer right there.

"What are you doing here, Earl?" she demands unpleasantly.

"What do you mean? Don't start that, Louisa. You know why I'm here."

It is lunchtime. Louisa and her crowd are allowed to go out at lunchtime. That is cool. I cannot wait until I'm in that school.

"I just thought—," I begin.

"*Don't* think that," she says, looking quickly around at the group of her friends gathering up behind her. Then she begins speaking in a rushed, desperate whisper. "Earl, Earl, why are you doing this to me?"

I can't understand her at all. I start to wonder if she is going nuts. People everywhere, it seems to me, are going nuts. "Louisa . . . you said, remember? You said it yourself, even though you didn't want to, about caring . . . for me. Caring, for *me*. Remember?"

"Sure, I remember," she says, but it simply doesn't appear that she does. She is scolding me. She is glowering at me.

Her friends are all around now. Males and females. Males and females and Wayne and all of them are older than me even if they don't look it, even if the years between us don't matter at all.

I feel so little. I feel so childish. Why is she doing this to me?

"Why are you doing this to me?" I ask.

"Why are you doing this to *me*?" she asks.

Somebody in the crowd, in the back, repeats the question.

"Shut up," Louisa shouts, to whoever it is, and I feel better for it. And I love her for it. This is all just a misunderstanding. She will see, and they will see now this is all a misunderstanding. I love her, that she knows, and that she's coming back and understanding.

She starts walking away. I hear the crunch-crunch of frozen snow under her feet like the hundreds of drummers in a parade, all banging away at once.

"No," I say, and start tailing after her, like a puppy.

"Please," she says, and the sound of it, the fullness and realness of it, stops me following. Stops me dead, here in the schoolyard where I don't belong, as she exits through the spiky iron gates.

She is begging me. That's the sound of it. Begging me to leave her alone.

To be begged for that. How sad and low a creature must you be? To be begged for that.

I can feel it in my side, like my appendix, my spleen, whatever, has grown talons and will claw its way out no matter what.

"You *lied* to me!" I shout, and if I didn't have the attention of the whole school population before, I probably do now.

"I *never*!" she shouts back, and stops.

We have reached a weird and scary situation, where we have both stopped to confront each other, without facing each other. I am staring at her back. Lots of people are filing past us, on the way to the sub shops and greasy spoons and corner stores and supermarkets of the area, where the big kids get to go at lunchtime, get to make their decisions, get to lead their lives. Lots are filing past politely, lots more are not.

"You said you care," I say, shouting less, shouting still.

"I *care*," she says, much more quietly, and her voice is cracking.

I wait for more. I have a full steam of *this better be good* building up because I am sure this is where she must explain, where she must make good, where she must make up for what she has been doing to me.

There is no more. I watch Louisa's back. I watch it as I have watched it for a long time now, as I have watched her back, and her nose and her hands, for a long time now.

It is so cold here. It is fifty million degrees below

zero. Why would anybody hang laundry in this weather?

Her shoulders shake. Another girl goes over, puts an arm around her, and they go.

Louisa goes.

I cannot believe it. I cannot believe this is happening. It was not supposed to happen.

The only things that happen anymore are the things that are not supposed to happen.

"Yo."

I was not even aware of Wayne coming up to me. Even now, as he speaks, I cannot remove my eyes from Louisa. She is leaving.

"What?" I say.

"This show is over, all right? You are finished here. You leave her alone, you got it, junior?"

He is right at my ear. I turn my head robotically, to three o'clock. All I do is stare.

"Don't even think about it, big man," he says, but his voice isn't as sure as his words. "I got friends now. And as far as I can see, you do not."

People always think they know. They never do, though. Never, ever do. Every time people think they know, they get it dead wrong.

I turn back and watch the last of Louisa. She has friends close at her shoulder at either side now, like an honor guard. Like a bodyguard.

"Is there a place around here for beer?" I ask Wayne.

Three tall cans of malt liquor should not be that much, for a big body. It is all about the amount of blood you have. The bigger you are, the more blood you have, so the less the alcohol can take up in your blood. That's the way it works.

So three cans spread over six feet whatever, and two hundred pounds and whatever, shouldn't dent a guy all that much.

"Listen, take some advice," Wayne says as he leans back over the front seat of the car. The car is a Volvo with about a million miles on the clock and the body and a million dog hairs on the seats. The driver is one of Wayne's friends, and I don't know his name, and I don't care to ask it and he doesn't care to offer it. Beside me in the back is another one of Wayne's friends, and even if I did care who he was it would not matter, because he is asleep. We are in the parking lot of MacCallum's Liquors and I feel sick, but not quite puke-sick.

"No," I say. "I don't want advice."

"See," Wayne says smartly before taking a long drink of the Southern Comfort he had me buy. "See,

Earl, that's why you never get anywhere, because you don't take advice. That's why you're still a kid on the inside even though you're like a giant on the outside."

"I'm not a kid," I say. "Shut up."

"So listen," he says anyway. "The advice is, you should stop acting like a freak."

I assume the look I fix on him now is an unfriendly look, possibly even a hostile look, because I see him lean ever so slightly away from me. I check by edging sideways and looking into the rearview mirror.

I hardly recognize myself. The eyes are all squinted up, there are deep angry lines zigging across the forehead, and the mouth is curled into both a grimace and a smile.

But I don't adjust it.

"I am not a freak," I say calmly.

"Well," the driver says, and right away I'm thinking, who asked him? "Well, you look like a freak, and you act like a—"

I lean calmly forward.

Smack. I aim for the mouth, and I hit the mouth.

I shut the mouth.

Nobody says boo.

The driver reaches a couple of fingers to his lip, which is already a little puffy but is not bleeding.

I tear open my fourth malt liquor, which is still okay, because of all my blood. It spritzes me from up under my chin, because it's between my legs, and because it's been upset. I take a long, long drink of it.

"If I may say so," Wayne says, from a spot close enough to the windshield that I'd really have to reach to get him, "you don't really get anywhere being all scary. And if you don't stop bothering Louisa . . ."

I don't even hear him now.

And I don't see him. I don't see anything at all outside of a narrow tube of vision that shoots straight from my own bleary eyes, through the window, across the parking lot, to the wide-open automatic glass door that lets people out of the back door of MacCallum's Liquors into the rotten frozen pointless endless winter out here.

Right this minute it lets two people out. One of them is my dad.

The woman who is holding his hand, I don't know.

I have a sensation like falling, fast. Falling down a shaft because I stepped out, because I was certain there was an elevator but there wasn't. Falling fast and hard and I can see nothing clearly as it all whooshes upward past me and I shoot downward through the shaft, through the ground, through everywhere, on my way to nowhere.

My can drops out of my hand, onto the floor of the car. I open the door and scramble out.

"Heeyyy," I call across the lot, marching his way. "Hey, Dad," I say.

His hand pulls away from hers as if it were an electric cattle prod. He has a bottle in a bag under his arm and now he tucks it in close like a football, like I'm the linebacker he's got to get past for the touchdown. The woman, who is about my mother's age, and about my mother's height and complexion and hair but is in no other way anything like my mother, looks suddenly horrified. She looks briefly to me, then back to him.

"Earl," he says, first desperate, then, "Earl," trying hard to cool it down. They veer away from me and toward his car as he speaks. "Listen, son, listen, we can talk, we should talk. Wait right here . . ."

I'm not waiting anywhere. I hear Wayne calling from a distance behind me, he's a million miles behind me.

I am right up on the door of Dad's car as he tries to stuff her safely away, safely away from me, safely into some kind of time machine. I am too close to the door, though, right on top of them, so that getting her in there is like getting toothpaste back in the tube.

"Hi," I'm saying through the glass as she squeezes in. "Hi, I'm Earl."

Finally he muscles through, shuts the door, and squares up to me while the woman buries her face in her hands.

"You will understand, Earl. . . . We will talk, just me and my boy. . . . You will understand."

"I will not understand. We will not talk. *Just you and your boy?* What are you talking about? *Who* are you talking about? This isn't right, Dad. Remember *right*, Dad? Well this ain't it."

"You don't know . . ."

"I know what *you* know," I hear my voice way up there, really loud when I say this, then down, really low, broken, when I say this: "Dad."

"You don't know," he repeats.

"I know what you know," I repeat. *"I know what you taught me."* As I say it, I *thump* him, with my flat hand on his chest. It sounds like a kettledrum.

I thumped my dad. I look at my hand, like it's not mine. I'd have rather put that hand in a meat grinder, than ever use it on him for real.

Then I thump him again. I just about manage to keep my hand open when I do it. I feel my lip go all fat and quivery, but I stop it.

He suddenly goes frozen-faced, except for flaring

nostrils. "Earl?" he says gingerly, and with a hand clutching his chest. "You've been drinking, Earl. My God . . ."

"This is not right," I say, pointing at his car.

He has no answer. Not for this, not for anything.

He sighs, he looks at his feet, he kicks at ice and snow. He looks over his shoulder at the woman sitting in the passenger seat of the big Ford. The Moms seat. Then he looks back at me.

"We have to go home, son. We have to talk."

I say nothing. I wonder if it is possible to stare at a person as hard as I am staring at my father right now. I hope it isn't.

"Give me just a minute," he says, reaching to touch my cheek, but I pull away. "Okay," he says, nodding, "just a minute."

"Right," I say, giving him a minute. "I'll give you a minute," I say, backing away. "I'll give you a million minutes."

I run, then I run hard, as if what I have just done is rob the liquor store. Wayne is waiting about ten feet from the Volvo, then starts running with me, and we pile into the car as if we are in fact dirty bandits. The driver starts up instinctively, and we peel out of the lot, like dirty bandits.

"Who was that?" Wayne asks.

"Shut up," I say.

"Where we going?" the driver says.

"Just go. I'll show you," I say as we pass by the wildly waving middle-aged man rushing the side of the car, rushing up to my window with a face so red and so wet and so sad like so many faces are when it is winter like this and it just won't ever, ever end.

Even though it's not cold anymore. I am not cold at all, though the Volvo has no heat and the floorboards are rotted away and the air is blowing up through them. I am hot, flushed, my hands sweating, my brow sweating, my eyes sweating.

Together

IT IS MORE WINTER THAN EVER. IT IS MORNING, BUT IT is dark. Nasty, brutal winter-morning dark that won't lighten up just out of pure meanness.

I am freezing nearly to death when I wake up. I am lying on a pew about halfway between the altar and the rear exit to the church hall, my coat pulled tight around me but doing me no good just the same. My hands are so frosted over it looks as though I am wearing thin, sparkly pink gloves, even though I never wear gloves.

I lie here for a minute, and more minutes, after I have woken up. I feel so sick. My side is bursting, my head is throbbing with the rhythm and power of a heavyweight hitting a speed bag. It feels as if something the size of a pigeon is in my throat, and I wish

I could throw it up but I'm so choked up that breathing is labor.

I straighten up into sitting position, and everything feels so much worse. So I lie back down. I stay down, praying. I am praying. Praying to feel better, to survive, and to die. Praying everything and everybody I knew yesterday is gone today and I can just start over with new ones.

It is easily a half hour before I attempt to move again. My hands will not move. If I don't get going now, I may never. I straighten up, like before, feel horrible, like before, but stay upright this time.

I shouldn't have bothered.

Stupid. Stupid, stupid, what did I do? What did I think? Rules. Keep your rules. Never, never let people in. People destroy. This was perfect. This was life more than life was. People would have to murder this, and you knew it. People always do.

I look all around me, and I cannot believe that things have managed to get so much worse. They have finished it. They have finished it for good. I cannot believe I brought those slimes into my sanctuary.

Half of the pews have been ripped up from the floor, and then used as battering rams to smash up everything. There are holes in the walls big enough to walk through. The altar rail has been torn down, all the various pictures of the various gods who have been staring down over my shoulder for the past year have been splattered over, scratched away, or somehow filthed beyond recognition. Both the toilet and the little sink from the pastor's tiny, terrible bathroom are lying out here in the main body of the church, and the place reeks of things a church ought never to reek of.

The speaker's podium, where I stood, above the altar, above the congregation, above everything and above it all, has been toppled to the ground.

I can't even complain. This is what they do. This is what the Waynes of the world do. They just need the stupid Earls of the world to make it possible. And I sure did.

It is snowing outside, hard. I know because it is coming inside, through the walls, into neat little pyramids building up along the outer aisles of my church.

I get all the way up, rising more slowly than any Methuselah. My joints move as if they are being operated by remote control, and every motion is pain itself as I walk the walls, touching the walls, making my last circuit.

The plaques are still up. All fourteen of them,

bolted to the wall and hanging on for dear life. They are scratched, gouged, but unmoved. They couldn't get the Stations of the Cross down without taking the walls themselves down.

Jesus condemned. Jesus made to bear His cross. Falls first time. Meets His mother. Hi, Mother.

The story never changes.

Simon someone is made to bear the cross. Veronica someone wipes Jesus' face.

Jesus keeps falling, keeps getting up. Some people cry, some people don't. They strip Him, they nail Him, they put Him up, they take Him down, they put Him away.

He gets back up, eventually.

I make the full turn, stopping at every station, moving on. Then I make it half again. He falls, He meets His mother again. He falls again.

He keeps falling, keeps getting up.

"Stay down," I say, as I step through a big hole in the wall, out into it. "For God's sake, stay down."

I cannot believe the stupid laundry is still hanging on the stupid line. Little mountain ridges of snow and ice building up along the tops of shirts, in the crotches of upside-down pants, everything frozen completely to death.

"Where's Moms?" I ask, standing in the doorway, shaking uncontrollably. I want to stop, I want it to stop. I do not want him seeing me shaking, but there is no way to stop it.

He jumps up from the table, where he is sitting in front of a large dinner plate that is completely mounded over with cigarette butts.

"At the hospital, waiting," he says, rushing toward me, his arms wide, his face shattered like a broken-mirror image of himself. He has been up all night. He is greenish white. He shakes as much as I do.

I manage enough scoot to dodge him and keep the kitchen table between us.

"My God, Earl, come here," he says.

"I want my moms," I say.

"She'll be calling in ten minutes. She calls every ten minutes."

"How do you know it's her, if neither one of you says anything?"

"Please, Earl," he says, stepping right, around the table, as I step left. "I've been sick, waiting for you, I've been *dying* here without you."

"Good," I say, pointing at him with one thawing finger, "you do that."

He stops chasing. But he doesn't stop the rest of it.

"Love my boy," he says.

I close my eyes, and make fists.

The phone rings.

"He's here," Dad says, and I can hear the click of her hang-up before his mouth even closes.

We stand there, staring at each other.

"Love my boy," he says finally, sadly.

"Hate my dad," I say.

He inhales some strength. "Love my boy," he says.

"Ya, well, you love lots of people, don't you?"

He looks like he's taken a body blow. One step right.

One step left.

"No, actually," he says, "I don't."

He steps, I step. It becomes, now, not quite a dance, but a maypole procession. The two of us walk more or less continuously around the table, a slow-motion chase where nobody gains on anybody.

"Try to understand," he says.

"Shaltnot!" I yell.

"What?" He has become so sad, I cannot look at him. As he follows me around the table, his hands are outstretched. Like he's learning to walk, and I'm supposed to catch him.

To hell with that. Nobody's catching anybody here.

"There are rules! Thou Shaltnot covet, Dad. Remember? There are rules! Thou Shaltnot lie. Thou

174

Shaltnot steal, thou Shaltnot commit adultery . . . remember any of this?"

"Honor thy Father and thy Mother," he says, so weakly it's almost a joke, a brilliant, hysterical joke.

"They don't honor each *other*!" I scream, and punch the table hard enough to bounce his cigarette dish up and over.

He acts now like this is important. Like scooping up the mess of ashes and papers and dead matches right this minute is central to the world spinning properly. He stops our circle dance, and begins collecting it all up in his hands.

Maybe he thinks I'm that stupid, that I will continue around and stumble into him and he will have me.

He is looking down, with great concentration, at his cleaning work.

"It was all right with your mother," he says softly.

For a second I can't even be sure that what he said was addressed to me.

"What?"

"I had no secrets from your mother. This was life now."

This was life now.

"This was life now?"

This was life now.

"As much as we could make it life."

I'm trying, my brain is trying, here and now, hard, as hard as I can, probably even too hard, to make sense. I am trying to pull every particle back into order just as foolishly as my dad over there is trying to get all those old spent incinerated ashes to collect back up into cigarettes again. The harder I try, the more it all blows around and smudges and scatters and the more it makes me rage.

"What are you talking about?" I scream. "Why did you do this to me? Why have you ruined everything in the world?"

He has done a mighty job of collecting all the stupid ashes, of smudging his hands, and his shirt, and his face, and now he straightens up, looking like some kind of psycho mime with sloppy grotesque makeup, and he drops the whole mess all over again.

He faces me.

"For you, Earl. We did everything for you. As much as we could, anyway, we did it for you.

"Or, anyway, we *thought* we were doing it for you. Maybe we were wrong."

There is no mistaking it now. He is crying. I have never seen it before, not at his own mother's funeral, not ever, and I do not want to see it now. I want to see him dead, maybe, but I don't want to see him cry. The tears and ashes mix and run and streak his face, and it is the most horrifying thing I have seen in the last few days, which means it is the most horrifying thing ever.

"You look stupid," I say. "Cut it out. Be a man."

He for sure seems like he didn't hear me, but there is no way he could have not. He comes around the table toward me, *again*. His arms are outstretched, *again*. He hasn't learned a thing.

I don't run away this time, though.

"It's not right, Dad," I say.

He nods, keeps coming.

"There's right and there's wrong, Dad."

He nods. He is wrapping his arms around me, and I could melt. I could melt right in there. I could lean into him and let his scratchy cheek rub against my scratchy cheek, the way we do, the way we did, the way I want, the way the world is supposed to be. I love his cheek, his feel and his smell. I love it all and I need it all and there's nothing I wouldn't have done every other day of my life for this very bit of stuff right here. He's my dad.

I stiff-arm him.

I grab the collar of his shirt with my left hand, hold him firmly at the end of my reach. I take my big right hand that he gave me, make it a rock. I look into his face and he looks into mine for an unbelievable, paralyzed second.

And I hit him, so hard, so impossibly hard.

He looks back up at me, his hands dropped to his sides. His cheek is split open at the bone. His left eye is all gone goofy, trying to fix on me but too loose in the socket. All wrong, all wrong. I hear myself crying, hear myself sobbing like a big stupid baby, I see my dad's face all streaky, red and black and greasy as he just hangs there, hands down, eyes up, and I pull back my fist and I'm going to hit him again.

"Earl!" Moms screams, banging the door off the wall as she throws it open. "Earl, Earl, Earl, *no*!"

Exile

I SPEND THE LAST COUPLE OF DAYS OF MY EXILE FROM school in the house. I have nowhere else to go and no desire to go there. Moms takes the days off from nursing other people to nurse me. She is there when I wake up in the morning and there when I go to bed at night, leaning close to my ear and reminding me to think thoughts like hearty soups.

"Like cream of chicken with rice," I say.

"Like broccoli-and-Stilton," she says.

In between those sleepings and wakings, we eat a lot of hearty soups. It smells so good here all the time that cats and dogs and squirrels and birds have the house surrounded waiting for the door to open.

We sit over all those big bowls of soup, me and Moms, dipping great chunks of crusty bread, scooping and dipping and finally swabbing until the bowls are spotless and shiny and ready for the next meal, and we tell each other all the true things we don't want to hear.

Bobby Norton comes to the door six times in two days. Five times I make Moms tell him to go away again. But he keeps at it. I wouldn't. I never would. This is something, then, to me, a remarkable something.

"You come back on Friday, right?" he asks, all excited like a kid while I watch a game show on TV.

"No," I say.

"It's Friday," he says, "I know it is."

"Friday's the meeting," I say. "Where I beg to come back. If they let me, I'm back Monday."

"Anyway," he says, clapping his little flippers like a seal and rubbing them together, "we're almost there."

We. I am still amazed by that.

I am shaking my head. But now he's watching the game show. I lean forward and shake my head more exaggerated to catch his eye.

"I can't be fighting anymore, Bob," I say. "If I come back, if they let me back, I can't be fighting. Not for you, not for anything."

He stares at me, like I'm stupid.

"I know that," he says, then looks away. He's trying

to do what I did, stare at the TV just to be looking somewhere else. "I can handle myself pretty good. I got pretty good while you were away. Had to. So I can handle myself, don't you worry.

"Long as you're there, is all. That's all I wanted, anyway."

Which is why he couldn't look at me. When people talk stupid they can't look at you, I've noticed.

"I'll take care of you, too, since you can't take care of yourself anymore."

He grins, looks slantwise at me without facing me. He wants me to talk. He wants to know what's going on. He doesn't know anything. Nobody knows anything.

I can say this. I can say if he ever invites me to his house to eat with his lame little Bobby Norton family again, then I'm going to go.

I don't say anything. We both watch the game show till it ends.

"Listen," he says, getting up to go, "you want to come to my house maybe and eat, this Saturday maybe, or Sunday, whichever?"

There it is. He's a good guy, Bob Norton.

"Thanks," I say, "but no."

I don't know. I don't know how it happens, why it happens, why it can't happen some other way. It just comes out, and stays out.

"Right," he says, and leaves without a fuss.

I am staring out my window as the time arrives. I stare out my window regularly, knowing as I do the times Louisa normally comes and goes. They can't take that away from me too, can they? I watch her, maybe like a sneaky, peepy freak, but it is only watching, it is polite, it is respectful and from a distance like it is supposed to be.

I am learning, possibly. I am learning the *Supposedtos.*

Anyway, she looks too. She tries to not, but I see her eyes. I have eyes and so does she. And I can see her look up toward me.

But I won't be confused. I can learn.

I say good-bye every time she goes. Good-bye, Louisa. But I stay away. Like I'm Supposedto.

Good-bye.

I am nervous as a cat when we drive into the school parking lot. There are lots of good reasons why I shouldn't care about any of this, shouldn't care what anybody thinks, shouldn't care whether I am wanted back or not.

And there are probably millions more why I

should be shaking and sweating over it, but I don't want to think about not one single one of them or I just might bolt out of here, or do something even more awful and permanent than that.

When we reach the little waiting area just outside the vice principal's office, the office I know so well, he is already there.

I knew he would be, but still. Still. When he jumps to his feet I am smothered from the inside, looking at him, and I know whatever anybody says, I will not be able to answer back.

He is clean shaven and dressed in a suit. I didn't know he had a suit. It smells like smoke.

His eye is swollen and maroon, and there is a chain of stitches in a vicious V-shape beneath it.

I am staring. I know I am staring, but there is nothing I can do.

Anyway, he is staring back, just as googly-eyed, at me.

"How are you?" Moms asks him in a soft and careful voice that I thought was only for me.

"Worse than I look," he says with a little laugh, "if you can believe."

Mrs. Vaz throws open her office door, and beckons us all in. She tries to look stern for an instant but I have never known her to hold that for more than a few seconds, and it is no different now. She gives me a quick, kind-of-secret smile.

Then she gets a load of Dad, and goes back to tough. She probably thinks she can tell a lot from the fathers' faces, and so she probably thinks she can know a lot about us. I think she probably can't even begin.

We file into her office, close the door behind us, and take the three seats in front of her desk. Moms, me, Dad. Dad, me, Moms.

Underneath the table line, Moms takes my hand. Dad takes my hand. My big ol' hands. It runs through me like a potent electrical charge, left to right to right to left again, causing my heart to jolt-jolt.

"Well," Mrs. Vaz begins cautiously, "what's new, Earl Pryor? Have we learned anything?"

Return

I LIKE MY FRIDAYS. FRIDAYS WHEN I GO STRAIGHT TO my dad's after school and he is waiting there without fail, leaning over the newspaper in a cloud of smoke, complaining about some athlete who makes too much money but is railing about things like having to carry his own luggage.

"That's just not right," he says, standing, not sitting, as he leans his palms flat on the table, surveying the newspaper all spread out like a general scanning a battlefield map.

I come up behind him, lean over his shoulder to see what he sees, and dig my chin into his shoulder like two heads on one body.

"Who the man?" he asks.

"Well, I guess that would be me, Dad. We getting a movie?"

"Is it Friday?" he asks. He pulls out some bills, and hands them up to me.

He sends me out with my orders, same as every Friday. I will get the bread and the milk, and the cigarettes, although lots of times now I will forget the cigarettes on purpose. I will get cream soda and Doritos, which are my idea and no surprise to anybody. And I will get us a movie.

We will eat and drink and watch our movie and I will wake up to my dad in the morning. At some point Moms will call to check in and check up. I will talk to her, and I will warm up, from my toes on up.

And Dad will talk to her. Maybe for a minute. Or for six.

I will wake up to my dad, at his place, three mornings, just as I will go to sleep to him three nights. Just like I will to Moms at her place, four mornings and four nights.

I can't complain. Because four-three is about as even as you're ever going to get, in a life divided up in sevens.